Hiawassee
Child of the Meadow

Hiawassee
Child of the Meadow

Marilyn Ann Haun

Doris Gaines Rapp

Daniel's House Publishing

Copyright 2014 Doris Gaines Rapp and Marilyn Ann Haun
This book is a work of historical-fiction.

Rachel Meadows (Hiawassee) was Marilyn Ann Haun's great-great-great grandmother. She really grew up with her Cherokee family in North Carolina. Before the great removal of the America Indians from the eastern states, she moved with her husband, Jacob Meadows, to his home of origin in Southern Indiana. His family had settled in the area when the territory was opened to white settlers. While there is no diary or written record of exact conversations, family stories and Cherokee legends tell the story of the woman who stayed in Indiana with her husband, even though his family, community and church rejected her. The historical information regarding Rachel Meadows is the historical account of the times and area in which she lived. These historical accounts support her need to flee North Carolina, before the government forced the eviction of all Indian tribes and relocated them to newly named Indian Territory in present day Oklahoma.

Daniel's House Publishing
P.O. Box 623
Huntington, Indiana 46750

Because of the dynamic nature of the Internet, any web addresses or links contained in this book may have changed since publication and may no longer be valid.

The cover art is **Reflection of Autumn** by Karen Noles, used here through a licensing agreement with the artist. All rights are reserved by the artist.

Library of Congress Control Number: 2014936716
ISBN: 978-0-9915033-1-5 (sc)
ISBN: 978-0-9915033-2-2 (iBook)

Table of Contents

Acknowledgments

I would like to thank Marilyn Haun for allowing me to write the wonderful story of her great-great-great-grandmother, Rachel Meadows. Her story could have been lost to future generations of family and friends. Rachel has a message for us today: we can adjust to our circumstances even if others don't accept us, by choosing balance rather than strife. Her story reminds us that we can find happiness if we lean on God for our strength.

I also give a big thank you to Jean Hayden. Your line editing was priceless. When I proof read, I see all the words I know I wrote, not the ones that appear on the page. Your talent is greatly appreciated. I was amused when I heard you refer to Hiawassee by saying, "She's my goddaughter!" When we hear her story, we all fall in love with Hiawassee.

The wonderful cover art is **Reflection of Autumn** by Karen Noles, a Montana artist, used here through a licensing agreement. All rights are reserved by the artist. Once I found the image of the lovely young Native American girl, I could find no other to match it. In my heart she represents Hiawassee. I hope you enjoy it as much as I. Visit her website at www.karennoles.com.

Doris Gaines Rapp

Dedication

Hiawassee – Child of the Meadow is dedicated to all the Native Americans who walked the long Trail of Tears from eastern United States all the way to the Indian Territory, now Oklahoma, and those who hid and remained hidden their entire lives. Hiawassee never ventured beyond her home and the protection of her husband, Jacob, and their sons. Although she remained in isolation, she did not choose anger. She maintained balance in her life by drawing on the peace she found in the arms of God.

Prologue

Into the mist of time, my heart reaches back to this free and cherished child of the Cherokee Nation. Buckskin clothes and moccasin feet, she ran along the trail next to the forest. No one remembers her Indian name but her story is re-told at the annual encampment of her people. I call her Hiawassee, because it means *meadow* in her native language. That is where she spent her days, gathering herbs and plants that healed her people. Her father I have named Ashwin, for he must have been like a Strong Horse to raise such a strong and free woman; her mother, Whistling Bird, since there were melodies in Hiawassee's heart.

Hiawassee, later named Rachel Meadows, was Marilyn Haun's distant great-great-great grandmother. Her life is woven into my memory like a dancing tribal shawl with threads of strength and those of tears, beads of love and those of sorrow. Every time I tell her story, her life and love fill me with joy.

Marilyn Ann Haun - Hiawassee's great-great-great granddaughter

Doris Gaines Rapp – Author - a new friend of Hiawassee (Rachel Meadows)

Hiawassee – Child of The Meadow   Rapp & Haun

Chapter 1
Hiawassee Learns the Fox's Wisdom

Circa 1829

"Hiawassee!" Whistling Bird called as she stood outside her small log cabin weaving a blanket on a twig loom.

"What is it Mama?" the girl answered. Her long black hair was drawn back into a single braid that hung down the back of her buckskin shirt and bounced as she ran along beside the stream. She carried a flat basket with plants she had gathered from the meadow, forest, and along the flowing waters near their village. Western North Carolina had been the homeland of the Cherokee people for more centuries than could be numbered. Hiawassee wondered if the wind knew how long they had been there.

"Did you gather any tassel flower?" her mother asked. "Little Beaver fell and cut his knee."

"Yes." The girl reached into her basket and pulled out the herb.

"I will make a poultice." Her mother took the plant and started to go into the cabin. "You can watch that the wind does not collapse the loom."

The young girl was happy to stay outside and watch for her mother. She loved the Blue Ridge, at whose feet they lodged. The blue breath from the Great Smoky Mountains had already gathered in the high canopy of trees above. To her mind, there was nothing more beautiful than the peaks and valleys of her ancestral home.

Suddenly, her eye caught the waning smoke of the

sacred fire as it ceased to rise from the large council house on a nearby mound. The fire that had burned forever was going out.

"Mama," she shrieked. "Come quick!"

Her mother dashed out of the lodge and into the clearing. "What is it?"

"The sacred fire!" she gasped as she pointed to the mound on which stood the council house with its roof of tree-bark shingles.

"Hiawassee," Whistling Bird ordered as she ran to the fading embers. "I will fan the flames, while you run to the forest and gather some dry twigs. Make sure they are not wet. You know the seven kinds of wood we use for the sacred fire." She looked right and left as she dashed toward the council house. There was no one around. The village was usually full of other women and children moving around.

Whistling Bird reached the council house and the sacred fire in a few leaps and fanned the flames with the tail of her shirt. The wind had been blowing all afternoon. Usually, no one person was responsible for the sacred fire. As people walked by, in and out of the council house, they tended the flame. But, no one was there. The village was empty, except for the eerie sound of the wind as it blew the leather door-flaps.

The War of 1812 had passed. The Indian Wars had been settled by treaty in the surrounding area. Still, the fear of war hung in the air like a black cloud that had touched the ground. Everyone felt it. The Cherokee did not want more fighting. They were one of the five peaceful tribes.

Hiawassee saw her mother fan the flames frantically as she went into the council house. Why did her mother look so worried?

Moments later she returned. "Here, Mama." The girl dropped the huge bundle of twigs and brush at her mother's feet. "I made sure it was dry." She selected a few of the driest pieces that seemed to have fire in their fibers. "I will help."

Together, they built a tepee shaped cluster of twigs and branches. Dried grasses were placed on the flame to allow the fire's temperature to rise and catch the larger pieces. They worked quickly and silently. Only their breathing and the sound of the wind was heard.

"Morningstar said they would be back to the village in a short time," Hiawassee gasped when she could finally step back and enjoy the blaze.

"Morningstar?" Whistling Bird quizzed. "You saw her?"

"Yes, they will be back into village soon."

"Where are they?"

"All of the women and children had hurried to the fields when the wind began to blow hard. One of the three sisters* needed their attention."

"What did they do to save the sister?"

"All of the women and children held hands and cir-cled the corn. They blocked the wind from tearing the ears from their stalks. They laughed and sang. Did you not hear them?"

"No," she sighed. Then she smiled into the wind when voices were heard floating into the village. Songs of harvest and praise drifted along on dancing notes. "There they are," she laughed.

"Hiawassee," her father called from the distant trail.

"Is the fire safe?" she asked her mother, anxious to run to meet her father, her uncle and the hunting party.

"Yes, small one. Go see if there is a rabbit you can bring to the pot," Whistling Bird laughed.

"Papa," Hiawassee called with glee as she ran down the path toward the hunting ground.

Ashwin strolled down the lane in buckskin leggings spotted with forest burs. He wore a jacket and turban to protect him from the cold that had blown in on the autumn leaves. "Be careful, little one or the burs will poke your skin."

Hiawassee jumped into her father's arms and buried her nose in the scent of the leather. "You were out longer this time," she complained.

"Did you miss me?"

"Yes, and I think Mama did too. We had to rescue the sacred fire at the counsel house, but she seemed worried about something. She seemed to be afraid to be alone. What is wrong, Papa?"

"Alone? How is it possible to be alone in the village?

"She did not see the rest of the village women hurry out to the fields to save the corn. She was putting a poultice on Little Beaver."

"What happened to him?" he asked.

"He just fell down." She looked her father in the eye. "Papa, I want to know. Why would Mama have been afraid?" she asked again.

"Well, if she saw no one in the village, she may have wondered if the wind had changed."

Hiawassee could feel his grip on her tighten. "What wind? What is happening?" she asked. Her smile dried into ashes.

"Come, let us sit," he said as he led Hiawassee to one of the seven arbors along the side of the council house. There was an arbor for each of the seven clans. "Four winters ago, our people established a capitol at New Echota. They wrote a constitution two summers later that declared the Cherokee to be a sovereign and independent nation. The Great Chief in Washington does not want to honor our sovereignty. The owl said to keep watch all night long."

"All night, but when would we sleep?" the girl gasped. "Is the owl ever wrong?"

"The owl and the cougar stayed awake all seven nights of creation. So today, they sleep by day and watch by night. They know what we miss while we sleep. This may not be a good time to slumber," he whispered softly in her ear.

"How do we keep watch on the Great Chief in Washington?" Concern creased her brow. Then she thought again. "Where is Washington?"

"Very far. Many days walk."

"What do we watch for?" she prodded on.

"I have heard talk of change," he said hesitantly.

"An agreement cannot be changed," she gasped. "Where is their honor?"

"I do not know, little one. But, we must watch and listen for the change. We must be careful of the cunning of men."

"Like the rabbit?"

"Yes, just like the rabbit," he laughed. "Rabbit lost his long tail, that he had bragged and bragged so much about, when he plotted to trick the fox out of a pair of beautiful tail combs," Ashwin agreed.

"Fox told Rabbit that he was fishing in the ice with his tail, so he could trade the fish in the Cherokee Village for a fine pair of tail combs. But, he had tricked Rabbit by tying fish to his tail before Rabbit got to the lake, to make him think he had caught them."

Then she laughed, "Cannot you just see beautiful combs hanging from Fox's tail?"

"That would be quite a sight," her father agreed. "So, when Fox went in for the night, Rabbit put his tail in the frozen lake and fished all night long so he could win the tail combs. When Fox came down to the lake in the morning, Rabbit was frozen by his tail to the fishing hole in the ice. Fox freed him, by kicking him out of the ice. Rabbit landed across the lake on the other side and only a very short tail remained. So, the Cherokee know not to brag about what God has given them, and to be very careful of those who call us friend when they are not."

"I will watch, Papa," Hiawassee assured her father. "I will watch."

*The three sisters: corn, beans, and squash

Chapter 2

Hiawassee is Warned of More Change

Circa 1837

"It will start, Hiawassee — soon," Ashwin warned. "Just as I said some years back. Now that you are a young woman, you must know."

"Know what, Father?" the girl asked, as she hung the herbs she had gathered on a drying rack near the cabin.

"Two winters ago, a small group of Cherokee Chiefs signed a paper with the white capitol. It erased an agreement they had made, the Treaty of New Echota. They would not honor that treaty anymore. They chose to exchange Cherokee land in the East for lands west of the great river. A hundred leaders of the people gave away the Cherokee land here in our mountains. They traded it for land in the Indian Territory."

"Indian Territory? Papa, what is the Indian Territory?" Hiawassee could not understand her father's words. The great Smoky Mountains had always been their mother earth.

"Oklahoma is a land far, far away, a place of native grasses that grow in the flat lands, around the foothills of the Ozark Mountains. But, the mist of our mountains will not go with us."

"But, the mist creates balance for the plants, the mountains and the rivers," she whispered. "Without balance, we will grow weak and sick. Why did the chiefs give it all away?"

"They should not have. They went against the will of the people. Chief John Ross had all the people sign a paper, asking the Senate in the White Capitol to not sign the new, unlawful treaty with their pens. But, they did. We have two years to leave our home, with the high mountains and fresh water, and move west."

"But, the Spirits live here. They whistle on the wind and sing me to sleep."

"I know." Ashwin smiled as he hugged her close to him.

"What about the plants and herbs that I gather in our meadow? How will Mama keep us well without our medicines?"

"Perhaps we will find new flowers and grasses in the new land," he patted her shoulder.

"But, we know what our people need. It is all here in our own meadow." Hiawassee pleaded. "Surely you have another plan."

"I cannot talk about it," he insisted. "Only those who are brave can know."

"I am brave, Papa. You always said I am braver than most boys. You can tell me."

"Let me tell you a different story," he began. "A long, long time ago, the plants and the animals could talk to each other. They shared everything. In the autumn, when the night air blew cold, and the earth prepared for winter, the birds would fly south where it was warm, and would return north in the spring."

"I have felt the change, and I have seen the birds take to the air in great numbers," she agreed.

"One autumn, Sparrow had broken his wing and could not fly south with his family. He told them to go ahead of him so they would be healthy and live. He would find shelter for the winter and see them again in the spring. He knew he would need help. He would have to find shelter from the bitter cold, or he would surely die.

"So he talked to his friends, the trees. First, he went to Oak. 'I am hurt and cannot fly south for the winter. I must find shelter from the cold. Can I live in your branches for the winter? When my family comes back, I can join them.'

"Oak had a hard and crusty bark. He did not think he would like the idea of someone living in his branches for many months. He told Sparrow, 'I do not want someone with me all the winter long. You must find someplace else to live while the snow and ice blow.' Poor Sparrow was so sad.

"But, he did not give up. Sparrow went to Maple and asked her. 'Please, I am hurt. I cannot fly south with my family. Can I live in your leaves and branches for the cold season where I can heal and be safe?'

"Maple was very polite but she answered, 'Sparrow, I am sorry. Winter is a long time to have someone living with me. Please, find someone else to give you shelter.'

"Sparrow was broken hearted. One more time, those he depended on, turned him away. He went to every tree he knew and asked them if he could find shelter for the winter with them. But, they all said no. Every tree-friend he had, turned their backs on him, except one.

"Sparrow went to Pine and said, 'I am hurt and cannot fly south for the cold season. I must find shelter. Please, may I spend the cold season with you?'

"Pine had no idea why anyone would want to live with her. She had no wide branches or broad leaves. She thought, of all of the trees, she was the least. She said, 'My leaves are not soft like Maple's. I have needles. But, I will share what I have with you.'

"Sparrow spent the entire winter with Pine. In her shelter, he healed. When the air grew warm again, and green began to sprout in the forest and meadow, Sparrow was able to fly. He greeted his family when they returned.

"When the Creator heard what had happened to

Sparrow and how his tree-friends rejected him, he called a great counsel. He said, 'You had so much, but you would not share even the smallest amount of all that you had with Sparrow, even though he needed your help. So, from this day on, when the winter season comes, you trees will lose all of your leaves. They will dry up like dust and die. Their crumbles will be blown away on the wind.'"

"I know what the story means, Papa. But, you are telling me another story inside this one." Hiawassee had memorized every story her father had told her over the seventeen years of her life. She knew they held great secrets of life. But the story of Sparrow and Pine sounded different.

"Our false brothers, who signed the treaty, did not act as friends of our people. They thought only of themselves and did not think about the young ones and the old mothers. There is now a mighty pine among our people. Though his skin is white, he hunts with your brothers and the other men. He is the best shot among them and wears the deer's hide as his clothing. He is loyal and honest."

"Yes, Papa, I know Jacob Meadows is a good man," Hiawassee said as she studied her father's face. What was he saying?

"We will not leave these woods and mountains, my daughter. But, it will be very dangerous. We might be caught. Some may be killed. When the time comes, Jacob will be your straight pine, and take you out of the valley, and into the homeland of his people. He will keep you safe, before the winter of the Cherokee bears down upon us."

"Take me away, Papa? What about you and Mama?" Her eyes welled up and overflowed the rims, until her face was streaked with tears.

"We will find shelter among the deepest trees in the forest, and in the whispering caves, where water flows cold and pure."

"Papa," she said as she squared her shoulders and stood tall. "I will do as you say. Will there be others like me in Jacob's homeland?"

"No, my daughter, there are none. But, you will have life in the shelter of his branches. He has asked if he can take you with him when they come and drive us off our land."

"Is there a meadow with flowers the color of the sky, grass that cools the feet and herbs that cure those who are sick?"

"Jacob tells me there is a fine meadow, with many streams and a forest like ours. There are no high mountains, but the hills role on to the sunset. You will be safe there. You watch for the signs of betrayal from the important men in Washington. Be on guard. Stay alert."

"You told me to watch, Papa. I will keep vigil. Then I will leave when the Cherokee winter comes."

~ ~ ~

Before they left North Carolina, before the Army came, Hiawassee and Jacob Meadows were married in a Cherokee ceremony. Clanship is determined by the women in Cherokee society, so both her mother and her oldest brother stood up with her in the center of the Council House. Her brother knew that he would be responsible for teaching Hiawassee's children in spiritual and religious matters, as was the traditional role of the oldest uncle in their community. Jacob's mother would have stood up with him, if he had been Cherokee.

Jacob presented deer meat to Hiawassee's family, to prove that he was a good hunter. She gave Jacob an ear of corn, which showed that she could tend a garden and prepare good food. Then the wedding party danced and feasted for hours. Hiawassee's heart sang.

Chapter 3
The Long and Dangerous Walk

Spring 1838

"You're doing well, Rachel," Jacob said as they walked through the thickest part of the forest. They made no sound. Each moccasin step was placed with the care of a skilled hunter. No twigs snapped or slapped at their ankles. A deer raised his antlered head and watched the two pass with a guarded glance. But, then he returned to the tender plants at his feet and those that hung from low hanging branches.

"Why do you have to call me Rachel, Jacob? My name is Hiawassee."

"You're leaving your life with your people behind. You will be living with me, in the world of the settlers." He pushed underbrush back with his foot and hacked at a branch with his knife.

"Do not hurt the trees, Jacob. We must leave it all in balance. The forest must not know we were here, once we pass."

"I know, Rachel. We will leave everything as we found it."

Hiawassee didn't talk about the sadness she felt inside. She would no longer hear her father's stories, gather herbs for her mother, or be taught by her uncle. She would not see her brothers and sisters, or hear her name spoken. She would be Rachel Meadows from that moment on. It was safer that way.

The Choctaw Tribe had already been removed from the east and relocated to the southwest. Every man, woman, child and elderly grandmother was forced to walk from the areas, later called Alabama, Mississippi and Louisiana, to the new Indian Territory in Oklahoma. Choctaw Chief Thomas Harkins, Nitikechi, told the Arkansas Gazette that the forced march west was a "trail of tears and death." News traveled fast from one Indian village to another.

Hiawassee knew the price that would be paid by those who would try to remain in the Blue Ridge. Her Cherokee tribesmen, who planned to hide in the Great Smoky Mountains of North Carolina and not be driven off the land, would be hunted by the Army. The government would also hire men who would be paid to capture any Indians that had escaped. The Indians would be brought into concentration camps at the U.S. Indian agency near Cleveland, Tennessee. From there they would be forced to walk west.

She knew that some would be captured and some would be killed. But, a group, however large or small, would remain, because they would not be moved. Even those who would successfully hide could still be tracked by bounty hunters, many years into the future. Men would hunt down all escaped members of the tribe and try to bring them to the authorities in exchange for their bounty.

Jacob stopped behind a clump of oak trees and held up his hand. Then he closed his fist and stood in silence. Hiawassee froze to the spot in which she stood. Her husband was their leader and had kept her safe so far. She would follow his lead. They were deep in the forest, with trees so close they had to walk around some clusters. The path that the bounty hunters would take was to the south of them, along a foot and wagon-worn path. But, Jacob had heard something. Who was in the forest with them?

Hiawassee pulled her blanket around her shoulders and waited. The silence was filled with the songs of birds, the rustling of leaves on the clear air and the babbling of a brook off to their right someplace. She knew all of the sounds, and longed to return the bird's call with one of her own. She did not.

The fragrance of meadow flowers floated into the forest and wrapped around them, as they stood in hushed silence. Hiawassee knew they must be nearly out of the dense acres of trees. The flowers she smelled did not grow in the heavily shaded areas of the woods. However, there was danger in exposure. When they came out of the forest and into the open space, what would protect her then?

They had left the Cherokee village in North Carolina days before. Her family and fellow tribesmen were still living in their cabins. She knew their time in the mist of the mountains was short. Soon, they would be rounded up like cattle in the fields. But, not Hiawassee. She had walked out of the Blue Ridge in the Smoky Mountains with Jacob Meadows.

He signaled for them to start walking again and Hiawassee followed. "Come, walk with me," he said as he motioned for Rachel to take her place at his side.

Together, they walked cautiously through the woods until they could feel the sunshine on their faces. They were at the clearing. Hiawassee wondered what her husband's family would think of his bringing an Indian home as his bride. Would they accept her?

Jacob looked to the right and left, but didn't move until he had scanned every spot in the treeless area ahead. A squirrel chattered in a tree behind them and a wolf howled in the hills. Beyond the grasses, and past the opposite woods, a stream of smoke rose above the tops of the trees. Even at such a distance, Hiawassee thought she could smell the rustic aroma of burning wood.

"We'll start into the opening, but we won't run. That will look suspicious. We'll casually stroll across the wide grass, like we're out for a walk. You wear my hat to cover your black braids, and tuck them up under the brim. If anyone is watching, they will be able to see my light colored hair." He looked into Rachel's eyes with the same love he had always offered, and took her by the hand.

Hiawassee could feel the warmth in his grasp and felt safe. Together, they walked out of the shelter of the woods. They were half way across the clearing when three horsemen rode up from the southeast. The pounding of the horses' hoofs vibrated the ground beneath their feet. Hiawassee remembered the joy she experienced when she felt the ground rumble at the return of her father's hunting party. She knew that the approaching men were not searching for game. Her heart pounded against the threatening sound of the hoofs. She too had gone with her father and uncle when they stalked the great bucks and knew how to not give off the scent of fear. She willed her breathing to slow down, which would slow the fearful beating of her heart.

"Where are you two goin'?" The biggest, burly man, with the sweaty hat and huge belly growled.

"We're going home, over there, near Heltonville. Can we help you men?" Jacob sounded calm and relaxed.

"Who's she?" The man asked as he pointed to Hiawassee.

"She's my wife, Rachel Meadows. I'm Jacob."

Each of the three wore a brace of pistols. A rifle was secured in the scabbard, near each man's knee. One of the men shifted in his saddle and the leather squeaked beneath him. "Why are you two dressed in buckskins? You look like dirty Injuns."

Jacob chuckled quietly. "You're right for that part, Mister. We probably are dirty. We've been in the woods looking for game and berries. The deer skins are comfortable." He looked at the three men and spoke to the smaller one. "I see you like a good buckskin jacket too. The skins are soft and pliable, aren't they?"

"I don't see any game or berries? You two must be the worst hunters and gatherers there are." One of the men seethed with squinty eyes.

"Actually, we started into these woods and then my wife began to feel sick. We'll walk on back home, and then I'll double back to the nearby forest and bring in some supper for the fire." Jacob smiled broadly, as if he were talking to good friends down on the corner in his hometown. He showed no fear.

"Don't you talk?" The big man hissed at Hiawassee.

"Maybe she don't know no English," one of the others taunted.

"Yes, of course I speak English." Rachel smiled back and used the very best white-man's accent she could imitate. "I just don't feel good. I'm sure you understand. I…" then she doubled over, as if she were going to throw up. She placed her hand on Jacob's arm to steady herself, just like one would do if she were really ill. "I…I'm sorry…I," she gasped between pretend gags, and covered her mouth.

"Are you going to throw up, lady?" the man asked. He wrinkled his nose with disgust and began to gag too.

"I'm sure you can see she is very sick." Jacob put his arm around his wife as she bent over in well-acted pain.

"I'm gettin' out of here," one man pulled on his horse's reigns. "In a minute, I'll be throwin' up with her."

The three glared at the pair, pulled up on their horse's reins to turn them around, and headed back in the direction from which they came.

"Are you feeling okay now?" Jacob asked as he watched the men disappear over the ridge.

"I am fine," she chuckled. "But, I almost made myself sick just chasing the men away."

"You always find a way out of a problem situation, Rachel."

"Hiawassee," she repeated. "I am Hiawassee, Jacob."

"Only in your heart, Rachel. To the world of the settlers, you are Rachel Meadows."

Chapter 4
Jacob's Family Turn Their Back

"The meadow is beautiful, Jacob, just as you said." Hiawassee smiled as she looked across the sweeping grasses that met the far woods and lined the trees with wildflowers.

"Just as I remembered," he said. He looked toward the thin stream of smoke that lifted above a far off home.

"Will they be good to me?" Hiawassee asked as she took in her surroundings. Her eyes caught sight of a small stream of water that ran through the valley. She smiled.

"I see you noticed the *crick*," Jacob said as they started to move toward the house. "The water is pure and clear." He took a few steps and then stopped. "I don't know how they will treat you, Rachel. My parents are good people, and very active in their church."

"They will be surprised to see you in buckskins," she said. But, she really meant, that his parents would be stunned to see him in Indian clothing.

"I know," he whispered. He took Hiawassee by the hand and led her to a fallen tree that made a perfect bench. "Sit. There are things you must know."

Hiawassee removed the pack she carried on her shoulder and sat beside him on the log. "What is it, Jacob?"

"My parents came into Indiana from Kentucky, and before that, Virginia. My father, Israel, was a soldier in the Revolutionary War. Rachel, he was also a sharp shooter in the Indian Wars, and killed many natives in his area. So many Indians died, they described the area as 'the dark and bloody ground.' Daniel Boone, the frontiersman who opened up Kentucky for the settlers, bought and sold claims to tens of thousands of acres of land. My father was able to get one of those claims, because of his part in acquiring the land from the Indians."

"Did my father know of this?" Hiawassee asked. Her voice was soft and shaking.

"Yes. I told him of the part my family played in the Indian wars."

"I know both sides were hurt. Many from my tribe were killed too," she agreed. "When you came into our village and lived with us, you brought the mission message of Jesus. You helped us and hunted with our men. You are not one of the Indian fighters. You are Jacob."

"I can tell you this. My parents are very religious people. And, they love me very much."

"Of course they do," Hiawassee laughed. "You are their baby."

"Yes, I am," he laughed and his cheeks looked warm. "I was born twenty-three years ago, on July 1, 1813, and I'm still the baby," he laughed. "They are leaders in their Mormon Church, and in the community. My mother stays very close to her beliefs, to the point of being rigid. Like a pillar of stone, she doesn't bend. She will not welcome an Indian into her home." His eyes looked down with emotion and he changed to another topic. Rachel heard him but said nothing. "My father is a very good farmer, but he cannot read. Mother can, so she handles the house and farm accounts."

"She is good with numbers and words, but is she good with people?" Hiawassee understood the difference between being a reader and one who understands what they read. "Would she teach me to read?"

"No Rachel. I don't think she will," Jacob said. "But, I will teach you."

They walked on in silence, each with their eyes fixed on the house across the way. Hiawassee smiled as they approached a red bud tree near the Meadows' home. "Jacob, the tree is beautiful. Did your father plant it?"

"Yes, my mother likes the red bud as much as you do."

The house was close enough for them to see the curtain at the window move, as it was being pulled to the side. The front door opened and a small woman stepped out onto the wood plank porch.

"Jacob?" the woman gasped as tears filled her eyes. "It is you! I thought it was."

"Hello Mother." He smiled broadly and gave her a hearty hug. It had been a long time since he had left to begin his mission trip.

"You have been gone three years, Jacob. You were supposed to go on your mission journey that would have lasted two years. Where have you been?" Then she stepped back and looked at the hand-sewn buckskin britches and shirt. "Jacob, why…what are you wearing?"

"I've been in North Carolina, Mother, living with the Cherokee. My mission was with them, in their village. I've helped in hunting game and making sure there is food on their fires and hides on their drying racks. You know I'm a good shot."

"Yes, yes of course. But Jacob, I don't understand. You have been living with the Indians?" Her face was ashen and her mouth turned down. She folded her arms tightly around her body and began to rock on her heels.

"The young men of our church go out and bring the message of Jesus to people far and near. Are we not supposed to tell the Indians of God's love?" Jacob sat on the edge of the porch and motioned for Rachel to sit beside him.

"Have you forgotten? Your father fought in the Indian Wars. Jacob, you know that." She had lowered her voice to a whisper. So far, she had not looked at Hiawassee.

"I know Mother. But, the Cherokee tribe is, and has been, peaceful. They are a wonderful people, and I chose to claim them for my people." He said no more for a moment. Rachel sat down on the edge of the porch in silence.

In her heart, Hiawassee heard the words of rejection and disgust from Jacob's mother. Was not God the God of all?

"Jacob," his mother breathed out slowly, "who is this girl, this Indian woman?"

"This is Rachel, Mother. She's my wife."

"Jacob," she cried out. "No! You haven't brought an Indian into our family."

"Yes, Mother. It is done. Her people are my people and my people are hers. Together, we bring balance to this new state." He said no more, but reached down, picked up Rachel's hand and held it in his. "There will be no more talk about it." He looked at Rachel and smiled. "And, we are hungry. Is there any extra food in the house?"

"I am a Christian woman," his mother began. Her head was held low and her teeth were clenched. "I can bring out some bread and some venison. But, that woman is not coming into my house." She turned and started toward the door.

"Mother—" Jacob's jaw dropped and his tone was crushed, like he had just been punched in the heart.

"No, Jacob," she turned around quickly and faced him. "You know you are always welcome in this house." She paused and looked at her hands. Then her eyes snapped up to Jacob's. "But, she is not."

"It's alright, Jacob. I can sleep in the woods. I love it there." Hiawassee would not allow there to be any anger in Jacob's family over her. "The balance must be maintained."

"Then, I'll stay with you," he insisted, with gentleness in his touch as he held her hand.

"Jacob…no. We haven't seen you in such a long time. Let her rest in the woods if she wants to, but you can sleep in the house with us. It'll be nice having you home."

"I'm not home alone, Mother. I have my wife with me. I'll stay with her, wherever she is welcome." His voice was not angry. However, his words sounded determined.

"Your father will be home for supper soon. He went into town. You can bring some food out to Rachel. I know Israel will be anxious to spend time with you. Please, come in." She started back toward the door.

"I will, sometime, but not tonight. If Rachel can't enter your home, I won't either. I won't leave her alone on her first night in a strange, new place."

His mother was silent for a moment. She waited with her head down as she stared at the porch floor. "The little cabin is empty. It only has two rooms. But, we started our home in that little space, before your father built this larger house. The roof is still good and the door string is strong. Just pull it inside and the door will stay closed to animals."

"Thank you, Mother," Jacob said eagerly as he jumped up to embrace her.

"Rachel," she began, but still would not meet her eyes, "you can plant flowers beside the door. The soil there is rich and will take to most any seed."

"Herbs too?" Hiawassee asked. "Are there herbs in the woods and near the streams? I could bring some up near the house, especially peppermint. It will make the path smell sweet."

"Yes, I suppose," the older woman answered quickly.

"And, I'll plant a dogwood tree for you. I know how much you like them." Jacob smiled at her, but there was sadness in his eyes. "I told your father I would protect you," he whispered. "I didn't know I would have to protect you from my own family."

"If the dogwood grows and blooms, there will be unity, a balance that will bring joy to my heart." She said no more. She would find a way to make a home in this new land called Indiana.

Chapter 5
The Little Cabin

Circa 1840

"Watch out for the loom," Hiawassee warned as Jacob came into the setting room from the bedroom. "I moved it a little, so the morning light would hit the shuttle. It was hard to see the warp threads in that dark corner." She pushed the wooden loom a little to make more room.

"It looks fine, Rachel." Jacob put his suit jacket on the back of a chair. "I like the loom there." He sniffed the air and closed his eyes. "It smells good. What's for breakfast?"

"I fixed bacon over the opened fire in the yard. It is wonderful out there this morning." The strap to her large apron slipped a little. She pushed it back and looked toward the door. "How many eggs do you want?"

"That's another thing. Sit down a minute, Honey."

Hiawassee slid onto a kitchen chair. "Is something wrong?"

"No, but this isn't North Carolina. The winters get cold here, and there's often a lot of snow. You remember the last two years and how the frigid winds blew. It can be really hard to cook over an outside fire in an Indiana winter. We'll have to do something else for your kitchen, at least for the coldest months. You'll have to have an indoor cooking area too."

"But Jacob, it is not because I have to be outside. I cook out there because I want to. You have already built a wonderful earthen oven into the little hill near the front door and I thank you for that." Hiawassee moved the platter of bacon she had prepared, a little closer to his plate. "I'll bring in the tea kettle. There is bread in the pie safe."

Hiawassee opened the door and stepped outside to the open fire. The smoke smelled sweet and nutty from the pecan embers that glowed in the fire pit. She picked up the tea kettle, from where it sat warming on top of a hot rock, with a folded, hand embroidered tea towel to protect her hand.

The weather had turned cooler in the last several weeks, but her feet were bare and her toes wiggled in the cool, damp leaves of autumn. She didn't even own shoes, and wore only moccasins when absolutely necessary. With the towel wrapped securely around the handle, she brought the kettle back in the house, poured Jacob a cup of hot water and one for herself. The fresh tea began to escape from the leaves and sent a fine steam into the air. She removed a loaf of bread from the double door, four-shelved pie safe that stood against the north wall, and brought Jacob a jar of jam her mother-in-law had given him.

"The bacon is crisp and good, Rachel," Jacob said as he crunched his teeth into a tasty browned piece. She watched as he slathered a generous amount of her sweet butter onto a thick slice of bread. "You know I have been drawing up plans for a great two-story house for you. It'll be the first brick home in the county. As the wife of a doctor, you deserve to live in a fine home."

"I know you have completed your medical studies Jacob. But, I have not learned whatever these people want me to know. When the house is finished, no one will stop by for a visit."

Jacob placed the bread on his plate and paused. "I know Rachel, and I'm sad for you. But, you will still have a fine parlor, with a pump organ and beautiful books."

"You have taught me well. I love my books." She took some bacon from the plate. "We have been in this cabin for two years now. I like it here. I do not need a larger home." The furniture was of simple pine. Jacob had promised to have fine furniture made in Kentucky for her, when the new house was built.

"When we have children," he laughed, "where will we put them?"

Hiawassee's eyes sparkled and her cheeks flushed. "We will find out soon, Jacob." She unfolded her napkin and placed it across her lap. "When my people arrive in Indiana for the annual encampment, I will have our first child to present to them."

"Rachel," Jacob leaped up and pulled her to her feet, twirling and dancing her across the floor. "A baby? That's wonderful!" Then he paused. "Maybe you'd better sit down," he laughed as he waltzed her over to her chair.

"I am fine," she laughed with the joy of her husband and their expected child.

Jacob paused for a moment and then knelt on one knee beside her. "Would you like to go to church with me this morning and thank God for our blessing?"

"But, Jacob, they will not let me in." Her eyes gazed upon the loneliness of her small room.

His smile faded a little but his voice was warm. "I know, but the Lord will know that you're there." He kissed her forehead and his tenderness filled her with joy.

"Honey," he added, "I know it's hard for you. The Indian Wars were so recent, the pain is still sharp and some wounds have not healed. Your rejection is not just because it's my family, or my church, or the people in this small community. The anger and hostility of the settlers for the Native people remains in every area of the East and Midwest, including this new state of Indiana. Many settlers are still afraid of your people. Honey, it won't always be that way. Someday, we will all live in peace. You know we couldn't have safely stayed in North Carolina. The Army would have soon rounded up all your people and forced them to walk hundreds of miles west. Your father didn't want that for you."

"Then I will continue to make this Indiana my home, even if the people do not accept me." Hiawassee stood up and removed the long bibbed apron she always wore. Her hands smoothed out the skirt of her dark calico print dress. Then, she smiled mischievously. "I will even wear my moccasins for you."

She slipped on the deer skin shoes she had made and beaded that she kept near the door. It was rare for her to put them on, so she didn't want to have to look for the soft slippers when she needed them. "Let me tidy my hair," she added and stepped into the bedroom.

Hiawassee looked at her image in her dressing mirror. She didn't do it often. It wasn't that she didn't care how she looked; it was that how she looked was not a source of pride.

With the comb Jacob had made for her out of a deer antler, she made sure the wisps near her face were held back. She secured them with the small silver pronged clips her mother had given her, when she left the Blue Ridge.

"I am ready, Jacob," she said as she came out of the bedroom. "I put a roast and vegetables in the clay pot, and set it on the embers when I went out for the kettle. It will cook slowly and be ready by lunch time."

"I know it'll be good, Rachel. It always is." He picked up his jacket from the back of the chair and slipped his arms through the sleeves. With a hug and a kiss on Rachel's cheek, they walked out to the carriage that he had hitched to the dapple grey. The horse was a high stepper and made a good, dependable filly for a doctor who was on-call at all hours of the day and night.

There was need for only one shod horse and one buggy to take to the lanes and country roads. Hiawassee didn't go anywhere without Jacob. It still wasn't safe for her to be out alone. Bounty hunters could appear from anywhere at any time. There was still a price on Hiawassee's head, as well as on all of her people who hid in the mountains and refused to be forced out of their tribal home.

The lane over to the church was lined with sweet flowers that reminded Hiawassee of home. They were beautiful beyond words. She closed her eyes and thought of the breathing trees of the Smoky Mountains, and the blankets of spring and autumn wildflowers that bloomed there, like a handmade quilt with a square for each blossom. She remembered the lady slipper orchids, columbine, jack-in-the-pulpits and glorious violets all waving in the clear air.

Once she and Jacob arrived at the church, the horse, Swanson, yielded to the pull of the bit in her mouth and slowed the buggy to a stop in front of the white, clapboard covered building. The last of the worshipers were just walking up the steps as Jacob helped Rachel from the carriage.

"Mornin' Dr. Meadows," one of the women waved.

"Good morning, Beth," he said as he took Rachel's arm and led her toward the door.

"Lovely day isn't it?" she asked politely but didn't look at Hiawassee.

At the door, Beth Richards stood in the partial opening and leaned on the opposite door jamb. "Will you be able to rest today? Anyone sick right now?"

"No, Beth. Everyone is pretty good. Your sister-in-law won't be havin' her baby for several months." He held Rachel's hand a little tighter. "We're going to be havin' a baby too."

"How nice for you. Will the baby have a white name or an Indian name?" She asked as she kept her nose up and her eyes averted from Rachel.

"Our children will all have settler names, settler ways, and settler clothes." He looked at Beth squarely in the eye and lowered his voice. "But, he or she will be the best shot in Monroe County."

The Richards woman smiled an uncomfortable smile, like someone who had been caught with a mouth full of words that tasted of bitter butter. "I know you are the most skilled sharpshooter in these parts."

Hiawassee said nothing but continued toward the door. She kept her hand in Jacob's because she felt safe there.

Mrs. Richards maintained her position as guard at the church door. She didn't budge.

"Beth, we want to worship and give thanks for the blessing of the coming little one." Jacob's voice sounded disappointed and pleading.

"Jacob Meadows, you are a church leader. You speak out at the town meetings more than most. You know the rules." Still she didn't look at Rachel even once. It was like Hiawassee wasn't even there.

"Beth—"

The woman straightened her back like steel and lowered her voice to a raspy growl. "Jacob, that savage does not come into the sacred sanctuary of our Christian church."

Hiawassee brushed tears from her eyes with the fine linen handkerchief Jacob had brought her from the village. But all the lace and tatting Jacob could buy would not get her accepted as a lady in the church or community. "I'll be fine right here, Jacob. You know I would always rather be outside."

"Let's just go home then, Rachel," Jacob suggested.

"No, I can worship anywhere. You are a leader in this church. You are expected to be inside." She lowered her head, moved closer to Jacob and tugged at his hand. "You must make a way for our children to follow into the settler community. You must scout the trail." Hiawassee moved to the far edge of the front steps and sat down. While Jacob went inside, to praise the Lord in the fellowship of his church family, she removed her moccasins and set them beside her on the step.

From beyond the closed door, Hiawassee could hear the sweet sounds of music. The melodies from inside entered her heart and filled her with both joy and sorrow. She felt joy for the love of her God and her husband, sorrow because the fellowship of the believers was not open to her. She whispered the words in her head and tapped her fingers on her knee. She could hear the solemn prayers of petition and the joyous praises of blessings received. She imagined that the message of Jacob's coming child was received with joy and excitement.

She had decided. Her children would be of the church and of the community. Jacob had promised that the prejudice would not always be there. The Meadows children would be received and welcomed with eager smiles on their friends' faces. Christian churches would one day celebrate the presence of the Native Americans within their congregations and treat them as children of God, even if it was not true now.

Her heart welled up with tears, but she refused to let a drop fall. Her children would not sit on the steps outside the church sanctuary. They would not be shunned. She would make sure of that. Balance would be found and maintained.

Chapter 6
A Trip to Town

"Are you about ready?" Jacob asked as he gathered up his medical bag and started for the door.

"Yes, I am." Hiawassee walked out of the bedroom as she tucked her long black hair up on top of her head. "I can roll the money into the last bit of hair." She folded the money for the material for three new dresses and rolled the bills into her upswept locks and secured them with hairpins.

She found her moccasins by the door where she had left them and slipped her feet inside. "Are you calling on the Kruger family too? You have your bag."

"Yes, Carl Kruger died of typhoid fever last week. I want to check on his wife and children. You will have to stay in town. Since you're expecting our child, I don't want you to be around their home. I told Mrs. Kruger to scrub down everything in the house. I'm sure she has scoured the walls, the curtains, everything."

"I will shop for the dress material while you call on them," she agreed.

"Why don't you buy some light and bright fabrics this time, Rachel?" Jacob suggested.

"I do not think so." Her memory drifted back to the bright colors of the festive dresses of the other Cherokee women. Her favorite garment had been a hand-sewn buckskin shirt with a shawl of brown and turquois blue. But, she felt so sad so much of the time, alone and without her family around her that it was hard to think of joyful, bright clothing.

"I will think about it." She said no more.

The ride into the village was a wonderful slow trot. The colors of the trees and flowers they passed were brilliant, like the country scene of a masterpiece. Hiawassee knew the name of every bloom in the meadow. They were pieces of her heart.

Jacob pulled Swanson to a stop outside the mercantile, tied the reigns to the buggy whip and jumped down so he could come around and help Rachel out. "Take my hand," he said as he offered his assistance.

"Thank you, Jacob." Rachel stepped out of the carriage.

"I won't be long," he said as he got back into the buggy. She watched as he drove off.

Inside the mercantile, Beth Richards was helping Carrie Shade with a few pounds of sugar. She looked up and scowled.

"Good morning, ladies." Hiawassee walked over to the oil lamps that sat on a display table. They would need more lighting when the new house was finished. The lamps were nice. One had a sculpted area at the top of the holding stem below the wick. While she liked the lamp, Jacob had promised to take her to Kentucky. There she would have many pieces of furniture made to fit her new home and lamps that would go well with all of it.

"Put it down," Beth snapped at Rachel. "I don't want anything to get broken."

Hiawassee answered without looking at the two women. "Neither do I." She continued to hold the lamp in her hand and studied the design.

"Well, I never," Carrie turned up her nose and looked away.

"Where is Doctor Meadows, Rachel? You aren't usually in town alone." Beth handed Carrie the change from her purchase.

"He is seeing a patient's family," she said but spoke no more. Over on the far counter was a display of fancy perfume bottles, each with a different color of liquid. She lifted one of the decorative glass stoppers and let the scent float to her nose.

"I heard that you just burn sage in your fireplace. No need for expensive perfume when you can burn weeds."

"Herbs, Beth. I burn sage and other herbs."

"Does that keep away the evil spirits?" she taunted.

"There is no evil in our home," she said as she smiled sweetly. "But, if you need some, I will be happy to gather it for you." Hiawassee continued to sample the sweetness of the delicate bottle stoppers.

Mrs. Richards didn't answer her as another patron came into the store. "Good morning, Henry."

"Mornin' Beth." Then he saw Hiawassee and removed his hat. "Mrs. Meadows," he said and then put his hat back on.

"What can I get you?" Beth didn't look at Rachel but kept her focus on Henry.

"That's okay, Beth. Mrs. Meadows was here first."

"She doesn't know what she wants. She just touches everything in the store." Beth straightened her back and twisted the bun in her hair a little tighter.

"Maybe she just enjoys the good smellin' perfumes?" He looked over at Rachel. "That right?"

"Yes, some of them smell like wildflowers."

"I'm sure you would know about things that are wild," Beth snooted.

Hiawassee knew her meaning but chose to understand it differently. "The flowers that grow freely in the open meadow are some of the most beautiful, don't you think, Henry?"

"They sure are." He gathered up a ten pound sack of flour and hefted it up on the counter top. "My Helen sits on the porch in her rocker and watches the fields of blossoms blow in the breeze. In the early evenin' when the sun is still bright enough for her to see, she does her mendin' out there, or knits a sweater, and enjoys the good smells that come up the hill."

"Sounds wonderful, Henry." Hiawassee said as she walked over to a stack of books that must have just come into the store. She hadn't seen them before.

"I don't know who has time to just sit around and smell the air." Beth started an order sheet for Henry Beckman.

"My Helen certainly doesn't," Henry bristled. "Like I said, she never stops. She mends or knits or does fancy needle art. You have sold some of her pillowcases in here haven't you, Beth?"

"Yes," she blushed. She actually seemed to recognize how rude her words sounded by the color of her cheeks. Then she spoke to Rachel in a less biting tone with Henry in the store but her words still hurt. "Did you actually want something? Or, are you just gonna try to steal one of those books? You can't read."

"I came in to buy some new calico." Hiawassee walked over to the counter in front of bolts of colorful fabric.

"I'll be with you in a minute," Beth said as she finished the bill for Henry's flour.

"I'll be out of here in no time, Mrs. Meadows." Henry's voice was caring and polite. That was something Rachel didn't hear out in the community.

Hiawassee said nothing. She went back to the books and selected *The Adventures of Oliver Twist*. She read the first few pages and smiled. She would buy it as well and placed it with the fabric. Casually, she walked over and looked around at the newest brooms. She could make brooms that were sturdier and swept better than those she saw in the store. She had no need to tell Beth Richards that. It was enough that she knew it.

"Now," Beth hissed out kindness as Henry continued to hang around the store near the door. "You said fabric?" She brushed the book away from Rachel's reach. "What color of material did you have in mind?"

"The three bolts there at the bottom are nice." Hiawassee pointed to the stack of folded fabric behind the counter.

"They are quite dark, aren't they Rachel?" Beth said as she pulled the bolts off the shelf.

"I prefer the dark colors." Rachel ran her fingers over the surface of the material and tested it between her fingers. It was thick and sturdy. "I will take six yards of each of these."

"Rachel, eighteen yards?"

"Yes, I do not have time to sit around doing nothing. I will be sewing." She pulled the book over in front of her. "And then, I will read this new book."

Henry stood near the door and snickered.

"There were some strange men in town this mornin' early." Beth oozed with an over-dramatic tone of care, which Rachel knew she didn't mean.

Hiawassee's heart began to race. She remembered running through the woods in North Carolina as men on horses with barking dogs chased her and her brother back to their village. Her eyes darted from the Richards woman and over to Henry.

"They were just Elmer Fry's brother-in-law from Ohio

and his two grown boys. They're here visitin' for a piece while they decide if they want to move west into Indiana."

"Are you waiting for someone, Henry?" Beth asked. She sounded irritated that he was still in the store. A barking dog has to be careful when a muzzle is nearby.

"I'm waitin' for Jacob to come back." He smiled at Rachel. "I want to ask him somethin'."

"What?" Beth asked then pursed her mouth like she wished she hadn't said anything.

"I'm sure you wouldn't be interested in my borin' business," Henry grinned.

"Come over here, Rachel and I'll take your payment," the woman offered as she gathered the fabric pieces and went back to the cash box.

While Beth's back was turned to her, Hiawassee removed the money from the roles in her hair. Henry smiled, and then pointed out the door as Jacob pulled up.

"Glad to see you, Doc." He held the door open for him. "Your missus is buyin' some nice piece goods."

"So I see." Jacob walked over to the counter and picked up the pieces of fabric.

"Doctor," Beth spoke in a sympathetic tone, "she wants to buy this book too."

Jacob gritted his teeth, and then answered with all the kindness he could muster. "Rachel does like to read. Well, if that's what she wants, that's fine with me."

Beth was obviously agitated as she scratched at her hair again. This time some of the bun slipped a little and long strands of hair fell to her shoulders. "Didn't you have a question for Jacob, Henry?" Beth coaxed.

"Now that he's here and Mrs. Meadows has a safe way out of here, I believe I forgot what I was goin' to ask." He tipped his hat and opened the door.

"Thanks, Henry," Jacob offered his hand in friendship.

"Your Rachel's herbs helped my wife when she got that terrible burn from the fireplace last week," he whispered in Jacob's ear. "She's a fine woman."

Hiawassee heard every word and sheltered them in her heart.

Chapter 7
A Fine New House

Circa 1841

"I do not know if I can leave our little cabin, Jacob." Hiawassee ran her fingers over the rough-grained, hand-hewn mantle above the fireplace. "Even though I have walked up the hill many, many times, I have not made that house my home."

"I know Sweetheart, but, we need more space. You have a kitchen inside the house in the new place and room for our family." He put his hand on her shoulder. "We have a nice sitting area in the kitchen where we can all gather around in the evening. And, the parlor is just for you." He smiled broadly. "I am well aware that a Cherokee wife owns the house and all the land. I built it all for you, Rachel."

She laughed. "I like that you remember the Cherokee ways, Jacob." She looked toward the outside. "You know I want to be outside. Kitchen or not, I will still cook out in the open with my clay pots over the fire."

"If that's what you want, that's fine." He looked out the window and his eyes followed the path above the meadow to where their new two-story red brick home stood. It was the first brick house in the entire county. "I bought the land before I left on my mission trip. And, now it is yours."

"The tall windows, with the wavy glass, do gleam even from here Jacob. I like that."

"And, they open real easy to let the spring and summer air in, just the way you like it."

Rachel smiled. "What about the smoke house and

coop for chickens?"

"You saw that they were nearly finished when you walked over there the other day. You had staked out the dryin' house for your herbs and plotted out the underground cellars for roots and other storage." He put his arms around her. "With the baby due any day, those spaces and your garden can wait a little."

"No Jacob, I must have my red bud and dogwood trees by the porch before I will move in."

"Rachel, the trees are there already. I put them in place last evening, when I told you I had to go out for a while. I was goin' to surprise you, but if you won't let me help you walk over there, you can't see them," he laughed as he hugged her again. "Maybe I should drive you over in the buggy so you can save your energy."

"Jacob Meadows, I am not weak. I can walk up the hill to the new house." She picked up her gathering basket, her shawl and the new book she had bought at the mercantile.

"No, you are most certainly not weak. What you are is – ready for that baby to come." He gathered up Rachel's spinning wheel. "I do think I'll use the buggy, so we can take this along. I don't want to carry this thing the whole way."

"I know what you are doing, Husband. You are making sure I do not walk to the new house. You do remember, all I need to do to divorce you, is to put your clothes outside the door." She leaned on him a little as she started toward the door. "But, I do like having you around, so, I guess I can ride." She looked back at the two rooms she had called home since she and Jacob had walked into Indiana. She smiled again and closed the door.

Jacob had bought the land for the new house from the government for one hundred fifty dollars. His certificate dated the purchase as January 13, 1834 and was entered into Book One, page twenty, of the official book of deeds.

He helped her into the carriage and they trotted across the meadow. The scent of honeysuckle clung to the air and the chattering of squirrels provided some music for their ride.

"You said you planted the dogwood tree last evening, Jacob? But, it is already a good size." Hiawassee couldn't take her eyes from the tree Jacob had planted for her. "It is beautiful."

"I chose a nice one that had been growin' in a clearing in the woods. I wanted it to be big when I put it by the house for you." He helped her up the steps. "Two of my brothers helped with the tree. They brought your rocker, my chair and our bed to the house this morning. It won't be long until we have the rest of the furniture made in Kentucky, like we talked about."

"Just as soon as I can travel, we will do that. While I wait for the baby and the furniture, I can make the coverlets and linens."

Hiawassee stepped inside the door, just like the many other times when she had come to check on the progress of the house, but this time she was home. She removed her moccasins and placed them by the door. As she walked through the rooms, she inhaled the fragrance of the herbs Jacob had gathered and had placed in a pint jar for a bouquet. She was pleased with it all. There was a fine stone fireplace and hardwood floors in the huge kitchen/sitting room. To the right, double glass doors opened into a formal parlor. The floors were polished to a high shine.

"I'll put your loom and spinning wheel in the kitchen, here next to the fireplace. If you want one of them moved into the sitting room, I'll change that for you." He carried the wheel further into the room. "Do you want me to put this here?" He asked as he placed her spinning wheel near the side windows by the hand crafted kitchen dry sink.

"And, something else Rachel, when we get settled in, I'll get you that pump organ we talked about," he added.

"That would be wonderful Jacob. And, a violin. I would like to learn to play a fiddle." She walked over to the corner where cabinets clung to the wall, and opened each door and drawer, and smiled.

The fireplace in the kitchen was surrounded in red brick, like the exterior of the house. "I can cook in here when it rains or snows, I guess."

Jacob sat down in the overstuffed chair beside the front window and watched Rachel as she moved around in the house he had built for her. She placed both hands on the two glass paneled double-doors and opened them into what would come to be her only world. In that parlor, there was another fireplace to the left.

The cladding of the parlor fireplace was a deep green marble with a white marble mantle. "It looks like there are forest trees right here in my parlor." Rachel spoke with excitement and breathed in the aroma of pine from the fire Jacob had already laid. The embers were glowing as they burned.

"This is perfect," she said as she placed her Dickens book on the mantle. "We will have marble-top side tables made for the parlor," she whispered. This room would be her sanctuary.

"Whatever you want," Jacob smiled at her. "I only want to make you happy. It is your home."

"I know you do, Jacob." Then Hiawassee's eyes grew large and joy spread across her face, as a large, fluffy white cat tiptoed into the room.

"You'll have to name her." Jacob watched Rachel bend down to pick up the cat and smiled.

"She is beautiful." Hiawassee cradled the cat in her

arms and stroked the mountain of silky hair.

"Maybe a Cherokee name. Wesa might be good."

"Wesa means cat, you are right. But Jacob, there must not be any Indian stories around our children." Hiawassee only whispered with a sad but determined tone.

"But, they will have an Indian mother." Jacob said softly.

"Their future is in the settlers' world."

"Rachel, people cannot become what they're not," Jacob insisted.

"My father told me the Cherokee story of the bear." She went over to the mantle and smoothed the fine leather on her new book.

"A long time ago there was a Cherokee clan called the Ani-Tsa-gu-hi (Ahnee-Jah-goo-hee). They had a son who would go off in the woods from the early morning until late at night. The boy's parents pleaded with him to eat at their table and sleep in his bed. But, the boy said he had been in the woods too long to live in a house again.

"He stayed in the woods for longer and longer periods of time. His parents started to notice that he was growing hair on his body. He said there was a lot to eat in the forest and he did not have to work so hard for it. He said he had already changed a lot and would not be able to stay in the village. He wanted his parents to go into the woods with him. He said if they decided to come with him, they would first have to fast for seven days.

"His parents discussed it with the tribal elders and decided to fast. On the last morning, all of the boy's family followed him up the mountain and into the woods. Because they had not eaten any human food for a long time, they were changing too.

"The villagers sent a messenger to try to convince them to come back. When he got to them, the messenger saw that the boy and his family had turned into yonv(a) (bears). The bears told the messenger that they would be there for them. When the villagers got hungry they were to come into the woods and hunt for them. They should not worry about killing the bears because the bears would live on. They taught them a hunting song that the hunters still sing, and then they moved along. When the messenger looked back, he saw only a drove of bears walking into the woods."[1]

Hiawassee stood by the window and looked toward the woods. "That family changed because the parents were willing to not be who they were any longer. They knew it was best for them, so they could be a family in a new environment."

"Then the encampment of your people is welcome here every year. You can be *Hiawassee* for the entire time they are camped here. You can call the cat Wesa and the children can call her Cat or give her another name."

"I will call her Wesa only here in my sanctuary, my parlor. The children can call her Blossom because she looks like a dogwood bloom. I will present our children to my family one time, after each one is born. Then they will live in the village and be people of the village. I will be Hiawassee for a short time each year, but in my home and in our town, I will only be Rachel Meadows."

Chapter 8
A Stranger at the Door

"Wesa, sit in the window," Hiawassee said as the cat leaped to the window ledge in one bound. "If you do not move, you will get caught in the leash threads as I weave this bed-spread for the baby's room." The cat obeyed, leaped to the window, stretched out on the sill and prepared to bask in the morning sun.

Hiawassee passed the shuttle under the warp with the weft threads and smiled as the white-on-white pattern began to appear on the loom. Within the design, she wove some soft plump threads that created alternating rows of fuzzy soft-ness with the more reserved rows of tightly woven design. She would weave a large bedspread for Jacob and her bed in a few days. She was nearly finished with the baby's.

All of the pillowcases, tea towels and chair doilies had already been stitched. They waited the needle art that Hiawassee would apply to each one. Embroidered flowers on the bedding and fancy tea pots on the kitchen linen were what she had planned.

Wesa jumped down from the window sill and slowly wrapped her body around and about Hiawassee's legs. She ignored the cat at first as she relaxed and passed the time at the loom. Her baby would be coming soon and she practiced only those tasks that gave her peace and joy. She wanted to set a tone of harmony and balance for the coming of the child.

"Hello the house," a strange man's voice called from the front porch. "Is anyone home?"

Hiawassee paused at her weaving and waited. Jacob was not home. She never had any visitors or callers. She made no sound because…she was alone.

Suddenly, the latch rattled and the door flew open. "There ya are Missy," a slim, wiry, little rat of a man stood in her sitting room. "I smell coffee. Can ya spare a cup?"

"You have no right to come into my home," Hiawassee stated firmly yet politely. "I must ask you to leave." She stood but did not take a step into the kitchen area. "And, we do not drink coffee." The man stood near the opening into her parlor. Hiawassee felt trapped in the room.

"I'd say by that long braid of yours that it's you who have no rights here." He grinned through stained, scuzzy teeth.

Still she did not move. "If you will sit there at the table, I will bring some tea. There is still some hot water in the kettle"

The stranger backed off slowly and sat at the foot of the table. Rachel could feel his eyes. They were fixed on her.

Hiawassee slowly moved to the kitchen fireplace where the kettle waited on a warming brick by the side of the fire. She reached for a cup from the cupboard and poured it full. Then, she set the cup down in the middle of the table where she would be out of the man's reach.

"Carryin' that baby makes you look kinda pretty," he grinned. "When's it due?"

"Soon." She was uncomfortable with the stranger in the house. Jacob had said not to let anyone in and that was fine with her. She stayed away from strangers.

"Where's yur husband, Missy?" He questioned between sips of herbal tea.

"He will be right back," Hiawassee said but she really was not sure when Jacob would be home. Mable Thorp always took a long time to have her youngins.

"I can't guess why any man would leave a pretty little thing like you all alone. And, you being ready to have a baby and all." He grinned again, a fuzzy yellow grin.

"Well, he will be right back. You had better be on your way." Hiawassee thought of all the objects around her that she could use to protect herself if she needed to. The tool set beside the fireplace was her safest bet. The poker that stirred the hot coals would be perfect. The handle was long and would keep him farther away from her.

"You got anything to eat?" He started to stand up but Rachel quickly stopped him.

"I have some bread but you will have to stay seated. When people bounce up and down it makes me dizzy. Dizziness makes me throw up. You had better stay seated."

"Up-dump your stomach?' He curled up his nose in disgust. "Okay, just bring me some bread. Got any butter?"

She did not answer. She took the half loaf of bread wrapped in a clean tea towel from the pie safe and a long bread knife from the drawer.

The stranger stiffened when he saw the sharp blade in Rachel's hand. "Watch out with that knife, little Ma'am." He sat on the edge of his chair. "Now, put that back slowly."

She cut the bread and then wiped the crumbs from the knife and returned it to the drawer. Before she removed her hand from the utilities she nodded at the cupboard. "I have my special strawberry jam on the first shelf." As the man looked toward the cupboard she had nodded at, Rachel circled her fingers around a paring knife and slipped it into her apron pocket. "I just opened it this morning."

Calm, calm, Hiawassee repeated over and over in her mind. She felt the comfort of the knife blade in her pocket as she pulled a spoon from the drawer and put it into the preserves. Like keeping her eyes fixed on a prowling panther, she stared at the man who had his feet under her table. She placed the jar of jam near his right hand and backed up to her standing position beside the fire. She would not turn her back on danger.

"Help yourself and then leave." She put her hand to her mouth as though she were going to be sick.

"I'm in no hurry." He grabbed the bread and scooped a dollop of red into the center. He shoved a choking bite into his mouth and chewed in slobbery delight. "I'm happy to keep you company."

All she heard were the sounds of slurps and sips from the man's cup and the tapping of Wesa's toenails on the hardwood floors. She was careful not to put her hand into her pocket, so as not to draw attention to the knife she concealed.

"I've just been wandering around out here in the new state of Indiana and I've bumped into some mighty mean men." He held up his cup for a refill. "Did you know that some of those lyin', feather-wearin' Injuns hid like little boys when the Army came to clear them off settlers' land?"

Hiawassee was silent. Her heart began to pound and she could feel her baby stir. As in the past, she calmly breathed in through her nose and slowly exhaled through her mouth. As she slowed her breathing, the pounding that beat in her ears slowed.

"You seen any of those escaped Injuns anywhere around here?" he asked as he nibbled on the bread. "Those savages have a reward, a bounty, on each one of 'em. I sure could use some extra money right now. Haven't worked for a long time." He stared at Rachel's frontier calico dress and full apron. He looked over her hair and the braid that hung down with every strand of hair in place. Then he looked at her feet. "No shoes I see."

Her thoughts raced to her beaded moccasins that waited for her by the front door. She hoped he had not seen them when he came in.

"I do not wear shoes when I am in the house. Carrying this baby makes my feet swell. Then when I feel sick, like today, they only seem to swell more. Why do you suppose that is?" she asked as she gagged a little. "Sorry. You will have to go. I think I will throw up."

"You talk funny," he said as he studied her with squinted eyes.

"Do I?" she questioned. "I came from Italy when I was a little girl. I thought my accent was gone."

"You a I-talian? I thought that was black Injun hair," he growled and finished his tea.

Hiawassee remembered a phrase Jacob had taught her. "Io sono di roma, Italia."

"What you sayin'?" The man slid to the edge of his chair, like that panther that was ready to pounce. His anxious pose looked like he had lost control over the situation.

"I simply said I am from Rome, Italy." She looked away and then looked back. "You do not speak Italian?"

The man's chair hit the floor as he jumped to his feet. "You makin' fun of me?" he demanded.

"No," Rachel insisted.

He crossed the floor in three giant strides and grabbed her by the wrist as she raised it to protect her face. "What if I don't think you come from Italy or wherever?" He twisted her hand. "What ya think of that, Smarty."

"Let go of me," she demanded.

"What you gonna do? Throw up all over me?" He was so close Rachel could smell the foulness of his breath.

With her other hand, she reached across her middle to try to get to the knife in her pocket. She struggled but could not get it.

"Do you want me to part your hair for ya?" Jacob bellowed from the doorway, his rifle pointed directly at the man's head. "Or ya want to limp from a blown out knee for the rest of your life? Take your hands off my wife," he yelled in anger.

"I'm goin'. See? I'll just leave." The stranger quickly released Hiawassee's wrist and threw both of his hands in the air.

"Were you hurt, Rachel?" Jacob asked gently while in total control of the situation.

"No, Jacob. But I asked him to leave and he would not." She stayed where she was. She knew better than to get between a stranger and her sharp-shooter husband.

The man talked fast as he tried to inch his way toward the door. "She was very kind. She gave me some flavored tea and bread and the sweetest jam I ever ett."

"Did you eat all my good strawberry jelly?" Jacob sounded as disappointed as he was angry.

"No, no, Mister. I just had a couple spoonsful." He turned to Rachel. "Tell him, there's plenty left."

"There is more than half the jar still remaining," she smiled a little.

"Now, I'll just be on my way." The man continued to edge toward the door. All the way, he kept his eyes on the end of the rifle barrel. Then he added, "You have a very polite little I-talian wife there."

"She is my favorite Italian," Jacob agreed while he appeared to stifle a laugh. Then he warned, "I'll let you go this time. But, you better know, I'm the country doctor around here and I'm involved in local politics too. Folks wouldn't set too kindly with some stranger in town, up to no good and hurting the fine women around here."

"No Sir…yes Sir. I mean, I'll just be goin'. I'll get a ride with someone up to Indianapolis. Maybe I can get some work up there." He stumbled over his feet as he tried to walk backward while keeping a bead on the rifle.

"You be out of town by sundown. If you're still around, I'll have you thrown in jail," Jacob barked.

"Yes Sir, thank you, Sir." He pushed the door open then turned and tipped his hat at Rachel, "Ma'am."

Hiawassee ran into Jacob's arms and stayed there until she heard the last footfalls of the man's boots on the porch. "I am so glad you are home." She let out a long sigh, like she hadn't been breathing.

He kissed her forehead, and then said with certainty, "Tomorrow, you're going to learn to shoot a rifle and a handgun."

"Jacob, did you forget. I went hunting with my uncle and father a lot. I am a good shot with a bow and arrow, a rifle and a handgun. I just do not have one." She snuggled in his arms as close as she could get.

"By sundown tomorrow, you'll have one of everything. You must protect yourself. You don't have to be polite and you sure don't have to feed strangers my good bread and jam," he chuckled.

"But Jacob, the Cherokee treat the stranger as a friend and share whatever food they have," she reminded him.

"But, it is different in Indiana. Your tribe is not here and many braves aren't around to discourage a man like the one who just ran out of here. If outsiders knew you are Cherokee, there would be a bounty on your head. Tomorrow, you will have protection."

Chapter 9
A Settler Baby

"I'll get my mother to help us." Jacob placed a cool rag on Rachel's forehead. "Our baby will be here soon."

"I am not allowed in her house and she will not come into mine. No one is coming, Jacob." She squeezed his hand as she felt their baby move again. "If my mother lived nearby she or one of my relatives would be here."

"Then, I'll open the window so you can hear the birds sing." Jacob raised the sash and smiled. "Listen, the trees are full."

The room filled with the songs of birds of many kinds. In between her pains, Hiawassee whistled the bird's trill right back at them. In the upstairs bedroom, Rachel and Jacob could hear the flutter of wings in the trees that stood near the back of the house. They both laughed when a mocking bird seemed to challenge a sparrow as the two birds chattered and sang back and forth.

"Who will be the winner?" Hiawassee listened for the clear songs. She whistled again. "Maybe they will think I am a bird too and interrupt their competition."

"Rachel, look." Jacob suddenly laughed as he pointed through the open window.

"A hummingbird, Jacob, oh how beautiful! It has a ruby throat and its green feathers are wonderful. You know, a hummingbird will only stay around where there is harmony."

"There is balance and harmony wherever you are, Rachel." Jacob removed the compress from her forehead, dipped it again in fresh water and replaced it on her forehead.

"Do I bring peace to your life?" She asked and then waited for a labor pain to pass.

"Rachel, you know you do." His smile lit up the room for her.

"It is a perfect day today." She shifted on the bed pillows and tried to find a more comfortable spot.

"What do you think our child will become?" He reached for the drinking glass on the table beside the bed and offered her a sip. "Don't drink too much," he cautioned.

She paused and thought. "The child will be his own person."

"Or *her* own person," Jacob laughed.

"I want only one thing for our child. I want him or her to be accepted in your world. If they are going to thrive and survive in Indiana, they will have to be part of the settlers' world."

"They will be, and their children will be welcomed even more." Jacob assured her.

Hiawassee closed her eyes and thought of her village in North Carolina. She remembered the happy times when new babies were born to her clan family and friends. Everyone danced and sang with joy. There, in the quietness of her upstairs room, there was no singing or native dances, but there was Jacob and he would be enough.

No rain fell that day – the sky stayed clear and the air was fresh. The birds continued to provide a concert of song. Later that day, the first of seventeen children was born to Jacob and Rachel Meadows. All of them were both Cherokee and settler, and every one of them lived in the community of neighbors, church family and friends because Rachel chose harmony, balance and Christian forgiveness.

Chapter 10
The Encampment

1842

"Do you want me to stay with you, at least for tonight?" Jacob asked as he finished unloading Rachel's things from the wagon. "The baby is just a few months old."

It was September and Jacob had loaded Hiawassee's spinning wheel and loom so she could spend some time with her people at the Cherokee Annual Encampment. Now that they had arrived at the large clearing, he had asked again if she was ready to be away from home.

"The encampment lasts for many weeks. The baby is quite small. I can send a messenger if our child becomes sick. Besides, I can nurse the small one back to health with my herbs."

"I'll tend to my patients and come back in a few weeks to see you and the baby. I'd enjoy seeing my friends among your people. Don't forget, I lived among the tribe for three years. We hunted together and provided for the people."

"I would like to see you dance with the men at the encampment. Their fine feathers and paint make the movements so amazing. That would be wonderful," she said as she remembered seeing him participate in the men's activities when they were still in North Carolina.

"I think I could get a lot of points in a game of stick ball. My racket would send the ball to the top of the pole and hit that wooden fish as many times as the next man."

"I know that you can." She wrapped the blanket she

had made for the baby around her and gathered Sarah up in her arms.

Jacob carried Rachel's things to her teepee in several armloads. As he passed the blacksmith forge, he stopped.

"Little Beaver, will you watch out for Rachel for me until I get back? I always worry when she's out of my sight."

"Rachel?" he asked.

"You know who I mean — Hiawassee."

"Jacob, when she is with us, she is our sister again. We call her by her own name."

"I know Little Beaver. But, she is Rachel Meadows too."

"I heard my name," Rachel said as she came up to the men. Sarah was already fixed to a cradleboard and attached to Hiawassee's back.

"We were just talking about you." Jacob laughed, like one who had been caught gossiping. "I asked your brother to look after you."

"Jacob, what will I be doing? I have my loom. I will make spreads for the bedrooms and my spinning wheel will turn out the thread for them. I even brought my violin along and plan to sooth the little one to sleep by the pull of the bow." She patted her husband's arm. "It is Little Beaver who will need tending to if he plans to enter the tomahawk throwing contest," she laughed. "Make sure you are not gone too long. Little Beaver may need your medicine more than mine. You might have to stitch him up."

"I hope not," her brother laughed.

"Little Beaver," Hiawassee beamed as she turned the cradleboard slightly, "I present to you our first child, Sarah." As the oldest brother in her family, he was the uncle who would train her children in the art of hunting. It was he who would tell them the family stories.

"Don't forget," Jacob teased, "I'm a better shot than Little Beaver."

"The whole tribe knows that, Jacob," she said mischievously. "But, in Cherokee tradition, as I am sure you remember, it is the children's oldest uncle who trains them."

"Yes, I am, Tiny One," Little Beaver said as he stroked the infant's cheek. "But, I fear I will not be around you very much."

"Let us have no talk of sad separations," Rachel warned. "The encampment is a time of joy and celebration."

"Yes, it is," Little Beaver agreed and turned to Jacob. "Did you bring your rifle? The men are going hunting in a short time." He put his hammer beside the anvil and took off his big, long leather apron.

"I don't go anywhere without it," Jacob said, but his tone was serious. He nodded toward Rachel.

"Yes, Jacob." Hiawassee adjusted the cradleboard a little. "You could get us a fine deer. If you bring it down, I could have some of the hide."

"Are you alright?" He lifted the bottom of the cradle to ease some of the weight off her back.

"Yes, Jacob. I am fine."

"Hiawassee, you know that everything is shared equally by the tribe," Little Beaver reminded her.

"Of course," she agreed. Then Hiawassee looked out over the campsite from the east to the west. "Where is our mother?"

"She will be here soon." Little Beaver looked toward the east. His gaze seemed uneasy as his brow furrowed.

"What are you not telling me?" Her eyes darted in the same direction. No one was coming.

"Our mother was not feeling well when we left. She told us to come ahead and she would follow."

"How many are traveling with her?" Jacob asked. He raised the rifle in his hand and gripped the stock tighter.

"You left her behind?" Hiawassee could not believe what her brother had said.

"Since our father passed on, our brothers have not been more than a few yards from her. All four of them are with her, Hiawassee. You know they will not let any harm come to her."

"Were they able to buy enough ammunition?" Hiawassee asked but that was not her greatest concern.

"Yes," he assured her. Then he smiled. "We had to get some a little at a time. The Army is still afraid to arm the savages," he emphasized the word with clenched teeth. No one in the tribe was a savage. They were all peaceful.

"But, you did say, she is sick." Hiawassee put her hand up to shade her eyes so she could see her little brother clearly. "What is wrong?"

"She has been dizzy and sometimes it is hard for her to breathe," he explained.

"Does she still smoke her pipe?" Jacob asked. "We are noticing that some people who smoke tobacco can have breathing problems."

"Yes, she smokes a pipe," Little Beaver said.

"She'll probably be here soon. They have to travel slower because of her health," Jacob reminded her.

"Thank you for that Jacob. But, your face tells me you are as worried as I am."

"You know, she may have a respiratory disease, bronchitis or something like that. Maybe you can find some skunkcabbage." Jacob put his arm around her shoulder and kissed her forehead.

"It must be cooked. I can make a soup for her." She smiled at Jacob. She could do something and that brought fresh hope.

"We do not know when they will get here. Or, if they will arrive today." Little Beaver looked worried.

"I read every day about the God of heaven from Jacob's book. If we pray, and if the Lord of heaven does not need our mother there with him yet, he will make her strong enough to bring her here to us."

"Then, while you search for skunkcabbage, you pray for our mother, Hiawassee." Little Beaver touched her shoulder with love.

She did not know where the rest of her family was, or if they were stopped by the Army or bounty hunters, but she knew what she must do. She would pray during the entire time she searched for the herbs that would help her mother when she arrived.

The plants would grow low, among the wetlands. Hiawassee looked to the rolling hills. Then, she followed with her eyes, down to the lowest part where cattails stuck up like signposts, marking the spot where she should search. With the baby snuggly tucked to her back, she ran to the brown-topped stems.

Slowly, she walked barefoot through the wet, tall grasses, with a continual prayer in her heart. She smiled as she sniffed the air and wrinkled up her nose. *Phew! Skunkcabbage!*

She brought the herb back to the teepee that had been set up for her use. Among all the things she had brought, she drug out the big heavy pot for stews and soups. She quickly attached it to the hanging pole above the fire Little Beaver had already set up for her.

The hunting party returned with a fine deer. "That didn't take long," she smiled as she turned from the fire.

"Jacob was expert at the hunt, as usual," Little Beaver said as he raised his hands to honor the expert among them. "We will quickly dress the deer and bring you a piece of meat."

Soon, Hiawassee set about dropping venison meat into the pot. She let the meat mix with the fresh water she had added, and then began the joy of chopping herbs and vegetables for the soup she would make for her mother.

When the soup was done, Rachel swung the pot to the side, just over the edge of the fire. That kept it hot without boiling the flavor out of it.

Hiawassee heard the whimper of her babe and swung the cradle to the ground. While her infant's needs were tended to, she sat back on her haunches and watched the east.

Suddenly, there was movement in the trees beyond the camp. "Jacob, Little Beaver," she pointed in the direction of the travelers. One person was seated beside the wagon driver and others rode on horses. She shielded her eyes and waited.

As the travel party neared, she jumped to her feet, grabbed up the baby and ran to greet Whistling Bird and her family. With the grace of a young doe, she leaped up on the wheel of the stopped wagon and flew into her mother's arms.

"You are here now, Mama. I have cooked a healing soup and you will be well."

"Hiawassee," her mother called out to her. "You are with me again."

"Mama," she gleamed with pride. "I want to present to you, Sarah, your grandchild."

And so, Hiawassee presented the first of her children to her family at their annual encampment. She would not take Sarah back again. All of the children went to the encampment only once. They were children of another world.

Chapter 11
The House Becomes a Home

"What are you doing, Rachel?" Jacob came into the sitting room where Hiawassee sat at the table drawing.

"The baby is getting older, Jacob. She will need a much larger cradle very soon."

"She is certainly growing, isn't she?" He smoothed the soft hair on Sarah's head.

"I am designing a bed for her." Rachel sketched carefully on the papers Jacob had brought home from the general store.

"And, these other drawings?" He held them up, one at a time. "Rachel, these are wonderful."

"That set of sketches is for the furniture in the parlor." She saw Jacob study one in particular. "That one is the settee. It will have cherry wood trim. I know most furniture is walnut, but I love cherry." Her eyes danced with excitement.

"This is beautiful." He inspected it slowly. "The fabric is a little dark isn't it?"

Her expression fell a little. "I do not think so, Jacob. I want my parlor to be, proper. The black brocade will be fine."

"Proper doesn't have to be sober and sad, Honey."

"I am happy…with you, Jacob. My home brings me joy." She put her pencil down and placed her hand to her forehead. "But, here in Indiana there is no breath from the trees like in the high Blue Ridge Mountains." She looked out the window as though she were seeing another place in another time. "The mist of the Great Smokies always seemed to water my soul."

"Well, the lines you have drawn for the back of the sofa are graceful and lovely, almost like the waves of the sea or the lilt of a song. Those bolster pillows are great."

Her face lightened and she smiled. "Thank you."

"What about tables? Have you thought of any side table designs?"

"Yes," she leafed through the sketches in front of her, "I have drawn these." She withdrew a few drawings from the bottom of the pile.

"Rachel," Jacob sighed, "these are wonderful. The legs are graceful and the marble tops are sculpted like pieces of art."

"Do you really like them?" She beamed with the joy of making a home for her family.

"They are beautiful beyond words." He studied each in silence for a minute and then asked, "Have you thought of a secretary with a drop front desk?"

"No, I have not seen one of those."

"There is one in my parents' barn. Maybe—"

"Your mother is not going to give me a piece of furniture. She will not even talk to me."

"Well, now, listen to me." He smiled in a kidding tone. "She doesn't have to talk to either of us to give me my own property."

"Your property?" Hiawassee stopped from her drawing and looked up. "Is the secretary yours?"

"I found it in a store in Heltonville a long time ago. It was in poor repair but I always intended to fix it up and clean the finish." He poured a cup of tea from the kettle on the warming brick and sat down at the table.

"I do not know about that." Her brow furrowed as she thought of the turned backs and the silence she had experienced from her husband's people.

"Well, anyway, your furniture designs are wonderful. Do you want me to mail them to the furniture maker in Louisville, Kentucky for you tomorrow?" He sipped at the tea and let the hot liquid stay in his mouth before swallowing. Hiawassee always knew when Jacob really enjoyed the food and drink she prepared. He seemed to savor each bite and mouthful.

"I wish we could drive to Louisville and meet with the furniture maker ourselves." She gazed into the fire that smelled of herbs and sage.

"I know. But, Louisville is roughly seventy-six miles away. Sullivan can pull the buggy about eight miles an hour at a comfortable trot. That's nearly a ten-hour trip. It would take several days."

"I understand," she answered. "But, we walked farther than that when we walked from North Caroline."

"Now we have a baby." He looked at the sleeping bundle in the cradle she would soon outgrow.

"Yes, we do," Hiawassee smiled and tucked the blanket a little closer to the child's chin. "I would not risk taking her out of this valley. Please," she laughed, "mail the drawings to the designer. I have labeled everything well."

Hiawassee laid the sketches on a letter sheet, folded the papers and wrote the address of the furniture maker on the outside. Then she sealed the pages with sealing wax. "There." She handed the papers to Jacob. "How long do you think it will take for the furniture to arrive?"

"It may take weeks for the pieces to be made. Then, it'll take several days for them to be delivered by wagon."

"I can wait," Rachel said as she went to the pantry and took out a few jars of vegetables she had canned. "These will taste good for supper with the strawberries I gathered this morning."

The dinner was prepared, the table set and the meal spread out for eating. Jacob ate well but he didn't talk very much. He seemed to feel well enough as measured by the size of his appetite and he ate with a small smile at the corners of his mouth.

Weeks went by and the usual demands of the day unfolded. Hiawassee strapped the growing baby to the cradleboard, put her on her back and went into the woods and along the streams and meadows in search of herbs. She would use some for cooking and others she would give to Jacob for healing his patients.

Jacob prescribed the usual medications available in the general store: aspirin and healing salves. Stitches for open wounds and the setting of broken bones were all done in his office in town. He also used Rachel's herbs for soothing and healing.

Several weeks later, Hiawassee was working in her herb garden beside the house. She had found many plants and moved them into her plot near the orchard. As she stooped to weed stray shoots from her green plants she could feel the rumble of wagon wheels in the ground beneath her feet. Wesa, who had been creeping through the planted rows, stopped and seemed to feel the vibration as well.

"Wesa, you felt it too. There is someone coming and Jacob is not home." She gathered up her herb basket and looked toward the south. A cloud of road dust filtered through the trees as she hurried to the house.

Once inside, she closed the door and threw the latch. Hiawassee removed the cradleboard, carried it into the parlor with Sarah still secured and placed the child and the board in a dark corner. She eased out the loose third brick over and fifth up, from the left side of the fireplace and removed the small gun Jacob had trained her to use.

Hiawassee was a very serene person who brought only a sense of calm wherever she went, except in her husband's family. She had never been in their house but even a moccasin on the first step of the porch would have brought chaos, and she would have no part of that. But, with strangers approaching, she would protect her baby.

Thump, thump, thump. A heavy rap on the door sent a chill up her back. She held the pistol close to her chest and stood behind the parlor door, a whole room away from the outside entrance.

"Anyone home?" a man hollered from outside. Then another voice was added to the mystery.

"You mean we came all the way from Kentucky and now we have to wait 'til someone gets home?"

"Wait," Hiawassee called after the two men when she got to the door and saw them begin to climb back into the covered wagon. "Are you here with the furniture?"

"Yes Ma'am," one of the men answered. When she opened the door, the man didn't pause when he saw her, as many others had. The two men made no comment and asked no questions. She was not dressed in native clothes and she wore her hair up, not in a braid. In town, every time the people laid eyes on her, they acted as if they were seeing a Native American for the first time. It felt good to be seen like any other village woman.

"Please, bring the furniture in," she smiled but kept her fingers on the gun in her pocket.

"Where do you want them, lady?" One of them asked her as he walked around to the back of the wagon and began to unload the pieces.

"In the parlor," she said and nearly danced through the house. She hurried ahead of the men, quickly took little Sarah off the cradleboard, opened the window and slipped the board outside to a spot behind the bushes near the house. She wanted no evidence that an Eastern Cherokee lived there.

The men brought in the settee and two side chairs that were covered in beautiful black brocade and placed them where Rachel directed. The rose marble-top tables were set at each end of the couch. Then, she hurried and placed fine lace doilies on the tables. She had made them just for this use, before the sculpted glass oil lamps were placed on top.

"We are home," she whispered to the child she rocked in her arms.

The men placed an elegant rectangle Persian rug in the middle of the floor, gathered up all the blankets that had covered and protected the furniture and started for the door just as Jacob walked in.

He looked at the delivery wagon, the men who smiled at him and the pleased expression on his wife's face. There was no evidence of danger there and he appeared to relax.

"Thank you, gentlemen. I see that your boss received payment."

"We wouldn't be here if he didn't," the horse team driver said.

"Indeed," Jacob laughed. He and Rachel followed the men back outside and watched the wagon pull away.

"Come," Hiawassee coaxed as she took him by the hand. "See how beautiful it looks."

"I'll be there in just one minute. You go in and sit in one of your fine chairs. I want to get something from the barn."

"The barn? Jacob, I haven't been able to force that storage room door open."

"I'll check on it while I'm out there," he agreed as he turned and hurried toward the large out-building. Rachel went back in the house and sat in the rocker Jacob had made for her where she could rock the baby and see all of the new furniture before her.

"Stay there," Jacob called from the other room.

Hiawassee wondered but she would do as Jacob asked. She waited until she heard a different sound, as if he were dragging something heavy across the floor. When he cleared the door and came in full view of the parlor, she gasped in joy.

"Jacob, what have you got there?" She placed the baby in the larger cradle the men had delivered that she had already lined with the large pillow she had made and turned in stunned excitement.

"I told Mother I was going to work on that old secretary that I had stored in their shed. She asked why I wanted the broken piece. She said, 'You have a desk at the office.'" He pulled something all covered in burlap by the end of a huge feed sack for easy dragging. Once inside the parlor, he removed the coverings to reveal the project he had undertaken for her.

"Jacob, it is beautiful!" she gasped as she gazed at the tall piece that had book shelves above, a pull-down writing surface in the middle and drawers beneath. The new finish gleamed in the light from the western widows. "It is a wonderful surprise."

"I repaired all the joints and made sure it was solid before I refinished it." He gave her a hug, then stood back to see her face again. "I'm so glad you are surprised and that you like it. Where do you want me to put it?"

"I saved a place between the two front windows. There is space there and the writing desk will get good light," she laughed.

"You saved a place?" He threw his head back and joined in her fun. "You found it and made sure there would be space for it?"

"No Jacob. I just knew. You said that you would find a way to get it for me and I knew you would be good to your word."

"And my parents didn't say anything. My father even came out to the shed and watched me work on it from time to time." Jacob hugged her again. "Maybe they are warming up. Maybe they will be there for you too."

"It does not matter," she said as she went to the piece with the velvet-like finish, pulled down the lap desk and ran her fingers over the wood. "The only thing that matters is that you are there for me. I knew you would do as you promised."

Chapter 12
The Parlor

Circa 1854

"I'm glad you don't look very long at the weeds, Rachel," Jacob joked as he hitched the buggy to a post near the garden. "If you did, you'd have them growing as fast as all these flowers you've planted. Whatever you look at grows!"

Hiawassee smiled but did not say much. She was always quiet, but today she was even more so. She was thinking about the coverlet she was weaving for their newest baby, Meadows child "number seven."

"Are the older children home from school yet?" Jacob unhitched the horse from the buggy and started to lead her away.

"They are in the barn doing their chores. You will see them when you put up Cracker." Hiawassee stood up and sighed a little with her hand on her back. She watched as Jacob led Swanson's offspring away.

"Our baby is growing," Jacob laughed and Hiawassee felt the warmth of his smile. "Anytime you want to just stay in bed all day," he said, "or sit in the parlor with your feet up, you go right ahead."

"I could never stay in bed all day." Her mouth opened in surprise. "I have never even thought of such a thing."

"Wesa could sit on your lap, and the two of you could rock all evening," he suggested.

"I will enjoy my parlor." She removed the large sun bonnet from her head and the long cotton stockings she had slipped on her arms and pinned to her dress. Too much sun was not good for the skin.

That evening, after supper, Jacob stood up at the head of the table. "We will do all the dishes." He watched as two of his sons darted up from the table. "Whoa, you two. I said we will all do the dishes. First, you girls use your mama's best silver tea set and take a nice tray of tea and cookies to her in her parlor."

"Can we go into the parlor, Daddy?" The girls' eyes were large with amazement.

"This one time…maybe. Knock on the door and if Mama says you can bring the tray in, then take it in and put it on the low table in front of the settee."

The girls hurried around with the hot tea kettle and Mama's fancy silver tea service. They opened the cookie tin and took out two butter cookies they had helped her make the previous day.

"A tea party," they gasped. "I would never have believed it." Together they prepared everything and then knocked at the double doors that led to their mother's sanctuary.

"Yes?" Hiawassee asked when she heard the unusual sound of someone at her parlor door.

"We have a tea tray for you, Mama." They looked at each other in eager anticipation.

"Oh my," Rachel sat up straighter and smoothed her apron.

"Can we come in?" The girls both held their breath.

Nothing was said for a few seconds, then one word. "Yes."

One of the pair of giggling girls opened the doors and the other carried the tray into the room. They gazed around with wide, happy eyes. "Here, Mother."

"Sit down," Hiawassee pointed graciously to the two side chairs. "Are your hands clean? We do not want the fabric to get dirty."

"They're clean Mother," Sarah, the eldest, giggled. "We washed them before we touched the silver."

"Thank you, girls." Hiawassee smiled as she looked at the tray. "But, you only brought one tea cup and saucer."

"Can we have some too?" Rebecca threw her hand to her mouth.

"Yes, you can. Now, hurry with the other two cups and more cookies. But, be careful that you do not drop them." Hiawassee closed her Bible and laid it on the side table.

"You were reading, Mother?" Sarah looked around the room at her mother's pictures and books.

"Yes, I read the Bible every day and a section of the Book of Mormon."

"But Mama, you're not Mormon."

"I am not?" Rachel's eyebrow rose.

"You never attend the church. Why?"

"Sarah, I want only harmony. Let us not talk about sadness."

"Not going to church makes you sad, Mama?"

"Do you like the new needle work your daddy framed for me?" She pointed to the cloth full of wildflowers that hung on the wall.

"But Mama…"

"I brought the other tea cups and cookies, Mama," Rebecca said as she came into the room.

"Thank you," Rachel said as she began to pour the tea. She handed each of the girls a napkin and then the cookie plate.

"Mama," Sarah sipped her tea and studied her mother from over the top of her cup. "Would you tell us what it was like in your Cherokee village in North Carolina?"

"North Carolina?" Hiawassee deliberately danced over the question about her life as an Indian child. "Our village was at the foot of the Great Smoky Mountains in the Blue Ridge. They call it Smoky because the trees breathe and their breath causes a mist to hang over the forest and gather in the valleys like clouds that have kissed the ground."

"It sounds beautiful, Mother," Sarah sighed. "But, what about your family, your parents, your brothers and sisters? Tell us about them."

"Each one of you children was introduced to the family at the yearly encampment."

"Yes, Mother, but we were tiny babies. We haven't been back." Rebecca coaxed.

"And, you will not be back. You have seen the people from far away. Your father and brothers sit on the porch and hold their guns on the valley where we camp, so that we will be safe. Your future cannot be with the tribe. It is not safe for you."

"Why, Mama? What are you afraid of?" Sarah sounded disappointed. From the set of Rachel's jaw, it looked again like her mind would not be changed.

"I will not talk about the Trail of Tears, Sarah. It was a time of unspeakable heartbreak. And those who hunted us down were more savage than the men in our village. I want only harmony and balance in my home. My parlor is where I find peace, not old, lonely memories."

"But, Mama…" Sarah started again.

"Eat your cookie and sip your tea." Rachel waved off her daughter's questions.

The girls said no more until Sarah spoke in a whisper. "I can't hold back my curiosity any longer, Mama. We don't even know your name."

Hiawassee was silent for a moment. She thought of the dangers of her children identifying with the escaped and hidden Eastern Cherokee tribe. The people among the frothy mountains could not be their people. Finally she repeated what she had always said. "My name is Rachel Meadows."

Chapter 13
Life is Large

Circa 1866

"Come Mother, Hurry! Benjamin has been hurt!" Johnny started back out of the parlor, and then turned when Hiawassee didn't jump to her feet and follow. "No, Mother," he demanded. "You must come now!" It had been years since Rachel's parlor had been disturbed.

She looked up from her Bible as her youngest child, whom everyone called Indian John, much against her wishes, came running into her parlor. He didn't obey the rule about not disturbing her while she meditated. He burst into the room with a frantic call for help.

Hiawassee had lived in the fine brick home in the hills around Heltonville, Indiana with her husband and their seventeen children for many years. She spent her days in her herb garden gathering the proper combination of plants for her husband to use in his medical practice. She passed her evenings with the family over supper and the children's school lessons. Then, her parlor called to her for quiet thoughts, sweet music, and reading. She was not to be disturbed. What was different about this night?

Hiawassee got up from her comfortable chair and placed her Bible on the side table. In the kitchen, she grabbed up her shawl and threw it over her shoulders, lit a lantern and followed John out into the night.

Sarah was at the table reading when they hurried past. "What's wrong? What's going on?" she said as she jumped to her feet and followed them out into the starless barnyard.

Hiawassee's heart raced as she tried to keep up with the spry young boy who seemed to fly along the path toward the barn. Sarah was close behind. Where was Johnny going? What had happened?

John flung the barn door open, stepped over the threshold and onto the straw-scattered floor. He looked back only once. His mother was behind him.

The body of twelve year old Benjamin lay crumpled at the base of the wooden ladder that led to the hay-mow. A large puddle of deep red blood pooled under his head. He didn't appear to be breathing and neither did Johnny.

Hiawassee felt Benjamin's face, his hands and wrists. She bent low with her ear to his chest and listened. Her face was drawn with emotion. With Sarah's help, she reached down, gathered him up and carried the boy from the barn. His weight and size bent her body, but she slowly moved up the path and back into the house.

"I'll put him on the table, Son. Take the table cloth off," she said as she motioned for Sarah to flip the corner back. Sarah responded in shocked sorrow.

Hiawassee lowered Benjamin to the surface with gentleness. While she waited, she held the boy's body close to her own and rocked him slightly, as she had done when he was a baby.

Johnny hurried with the beautifully embroidered cloth and folded it carefully as his mother would expect. "I'll run and get Papa." Johnny spoke quickly and had already started for the door. "He stopped up at Grandma Meadows' house."

"There is no need to hurry. Benjamin has already gone to the Great Spirit, to God," she whispered as tears ran down her face. "There is nothing your daddy can do to stop what has already happened. You can bring water in the basin and a wash cloth. Then you can go fetch your father."

"What will you do, Mama?"

"I will wash my son, Johnny."

"But, Mama, use the herbs you give to Papa every day and make Benjamin well again. God took him away too soon."

"We are always taken away too soon, Son, if we measure our time on earth by our own desires. God's timing is different. It is a circle. That is the way of life. We are born, we live, we use up every moment of the time we are given, and we move on. It is a cycle and we are all bound by God's laws of the circle of life."

"Doesn't the Cherokee have any secret way of bringing Benjamin back?" Tears streamed down his cheeks and Johnny wiped them on the back of his shirt sleeve.

"We do not talk about Indian ways in this house. You know that, Johnny. Besides, the Cherokee believe that all must be in balance, at peace. How could a soul be at peace if it was brought back from the throne of Glory?" She dipped a corner of the cloth in the water Sarah had brought her and began to wash the boy's face.

"You read the Bible every day. Is that how you know about peace?" Johnny touched Benjamin's hand and pulled back.

"I have been taught about it all my life. You must find your own peace, Son." With the wet cloth in her hand, she rubbed a little soap into it, wrung out the excess and washed Benjamin's hands just as Jacob came into the house.

He threw his hand to his mouth to stifle a gasp. "What happened?" He hurried to his son and gathered him in his arms. Great sobs of grief rose up and spilled into the room.

"He fell, Papa," Johnny whispered.

"Why? Why wasn't he in bed?" Jacob laid the body down and brushed the hair from the boy's eyes.

"I was reading, Papa. I didn't even hear him sneak out," Sarah sobbed as she wiped tears from her face.

"He said Wesa-two was gonna have kittens," Johnny whispered. "He saw her jump up on the hay wagon, then into the hay-mow. He said she was making a bed up there for her and her kittens. He wanted to see them. I followed Benjamin into the barn. When he slipped on the top rung of the ladder, I screamed." Johnny's voice tightened with grief. "But, I couldn't catch him."

"Johnny, Son," Jacob's eyes closed with sorrow. Then a look of compassion washed over his face. "You couldn't have caught Benjamin. He is twelve years old. You are nine. He weighs twenty pounds more than you."

Johnny watched in silence for a moment and then he asked, "Why does he look so small up there on the table?" He started to cry again and hid his face in his hands.

"I don't know. He looks the same to me." Jacob offered words that were soothing and he tried to put his arm around his youngest one.

"No, he doesn't," Johnny protested as he folded his arms around himself. His dad reached for him but, he jerked away and slumped down on one of the chairs.

"Johnny Boy, try not to wake up your brothers and sisters." Jacob crouched down in front of him and took his hands in his. "They'll find out about Benjamin's accident tomorrow. Let them sleep tonight."

"But, Papa," he sobbed, "I don't think I'll ever be able to sleep again. I won't be able to say my prayers. If I don't say my prayers, I won't sleep."

"Why won't you be able to pray?" Jacob patted him on the cheek.

"Cause, I'd only want to pray that it didn't happen. But, it did."

"Wishing for things that could never happen, will only disappoint you twice," Jacob said as he peeked at his son through the spaces between the boy's fingers. "It disappoints when the thing you wish for doesn't happen. It disappoints again when you realize how foolish you were for wishing in the first place."

"Okay, if you say so, Papa." Johnny watched as his mother lovingly washed his brother's body. "You always say I'm supposed to learn something from everything that happens." Johnny looked over at Benjamin again. "I still think he looks smaller than he was."

"It is because our Benjamin is not here anymore." Rachel smiled at Johnny and smoothed his rumpled hair. Johnny reminded her of her brother, Little Beaver. "Benjamin's life was so full and big it filled out his body and made him so much larger when he was still with us."

"So, he was big when he was alive." Johnny seemed to think hard about what Rachel had said. Then, he added, "Life is a real thing isn't it? It even makes us heavier and taller." He smiled to himself and then added. "I guess that's because God is real too. We are bigger people when he lives inside."

Chapter 14
Rachel's Light Is Gone

1893

"I'm going huntin', Rachel," Jacob called to Hiawassee as she puttered in her greenhouse. She cleaned some clay pots and prepared them for spring. "I'll be back in a few hours."

"I will be here as always, Jacob," she laughed and looked up at him as he bent to kiss her forehead. He had nearly completed his seventy-ninth year. He was as strong as he had always been since the day he had walked into the Smoky Mountains and into her village so many years before.

She watched as he gathered up his hunting equipment from where he had placed it on the potting bench and stopped to talk to Johnny. "Some of your brothers are going with me. I need for you to stay here at the house, Son, and take care of your mother. Always make sure she has plenty of wood for the fire."

"You can count on me, Papa." Johnny patted his father on the back and sealed the agreement.

It was mid-morning when the Meadows hunting party returned with a fine male deer, a buck with six points on his antlers. The animal was tied across the back of a horse in order to transport it back to the farm.

"A six-pointer!" Hiawassee clapped her hands together as she came out of the house. She waved the tea towel she carried like a victory flag. "I see at least one pair of new moccasins."

"One pair? I see a store full," Jacob laughed. "What will you do with the rest of the hide? It's always yours."

"I will see. I know I could use another herb bag." She watched the boys carefully prepare the deer for removal from the back of the horse. "There is a lot of meat on him as well."

"Johnny, you can start the fire in the smokehouse. By the time it is hot enough, the first of the meat will be ready to be cured." Jacob waved as he began to guide the boys as they lifted the deer to a tall oak tree.

The barn yard buzzed with activity beneath a robin's-egg-blue winter sky. Rachel brushed fresh snow flakes from the porch with a sturdy broom, some of the sons were splitting wood for the fireplaces, several of the girls were beating holiday crumbs from the rugs as they hung on the clothes line after the Christmas feast a few days before, and the hunters were dressing out the deer. All were little vignettes below a clear sky, pictures of work and fun scattered all over the property.

The wind blew gently across the meadow and rustled small branches and twigs that had gathered beneath the trees. Colors of the sunlight caught freshly falling snow-flakes and danced like fireflies to unsung melodies. It was a perfect winter day.

They hoisted the deer up by rope-and-pulleys to hang from a frozen branch of the tall tree. It was the very same method for preparing the deer to be dressed out, as it had always been. The hide would be removed and then the meat. Even parts of the bone, the sinew, would be stripped off and used as sturdy string and bindings.

Then suddenly a scream pierced the heart of the day.

"Papa!" Johnny shouted over his brothers' scramble to help their father. "Mama, come help!"

Hiawassee had already dropped her broom and had

started down the porch steps. Her aging joints usually dictated her speed, but that day nothing would keep her from her husband.

Jacob's body lay on the cold ground under the broken limb from which the deer had hung. The huge animal pinned him to the dirt by its long antlers. Rachel got down on her knees and crawled on the ice-like pebbles around Jacob's body, quickly inspecting it from every angle. One of the longest antler points had pierced his lung.

Hiawassee ran to her drying room beside the greenhouse where her harvested herbs hung. She pulled down several kinds and hurried them to the kitchen to make a poultice. She poured hot water from the tea kettle, added the herbs and spread the moist paste onto a cheese cloth. With the medication in hand, she ran back to the foot of the tree to tend to her husband, her life.

"How are you Jacob?" She asked as she crept near his punctured body. "The deer will have to be lifted off of you." She struggled to fight back the tears that threatened to drown her in fear. "I know you are strong, but, you will probably get very dizzy and leave us for a while."

Jacob could not speak. There was no air coming from his lungs but he looked into Rachel's eyes and nodded.

"You boys secure the rope to the tree again and pull the deer off of your papa. I will have to apply the poultice very quickly, so work in a space where you are out of my way." She spoke swiftly and then said no more as one of their sons scrambled up the tree to reposition the rope. With weathered fingers, she pointed to one son after the other, to the deer, to the rope and to the tree. She counted to three on outstretched fingers and then gave a jerking motion with her closed fist. She watched in horror as the animal was yanked from her dear husband's body. It lifted him slightly off the ground and then dropped him once he was free. She fell down beside Jacob, tore open his shirt and expertly placed the poultice on his chest. With a sweeping motion of her arms, she instructed her boys to gather him up and carry him into the house.

Hiawassee hurried ahead of them, flung the door open and led the way up the stairs and into their bedroom. Rachel heard a deep and painful moan as Jacob was placed carefully on the bed. She quickly covered him with bed covers. "Warmth will help bring him back to us." She spoke almost to herself.

"We will get lunch around for the rest of the family," Sarah offered as she tapped her sister on the shoulder. She continued to stare at the limp body of their strong and hearty father.

"We have to do something," Rebecca added.

Hiawassee said nothing but looked up at them with a little smile. She stayed with Jacob all that day. Rachel changed the poultice often and she did not leave his side. Passages from the Bible gave her comfort and some of them she read aloud, whispering the words in his ear.

Rachel tried everything. Every herb, each touch, all of her known cures for illnesses were used, but he did not improve. A hole in his chest was not the same as a disease.

Jacob lived for six weeks and she stayed with him every moment. Late the last day, Rachel lifted her head from where she had laid it on the edge of the bed. Something was different. All night Jacob had struggled with every breath, but now, the struggle had stopped. Rachel touched his hand and caressed his cheeks, but he was gone. It was February 6, 1893. In six more months, he would have been eighty years old.

Hiawassee called in her children to say their goodbyes. Then, she prepared Jacob's body for burial.

The next day was not nearly as beautiful as the days before. The gray sky seemed to weep for the country doctor as they carried him to the church for the funeral service. The beauty of sparkling snow didn't even bless the day.

When they arrived at the church, Rachel and Jacob's children greeted all those who came to pay their respects. So many people rode in from the valleys and hillsides, the ridges and hollows that some had to stand at the back and along the sides of the sanctuary. No one looked at Rachel.

Hiawassee sat down on the snow dusted steps outside the church, tucked her coat under her dark blue calico print dress, pulled her pipe out of her pocket and lit a match. From the other side of the door, she listened to the sounds of the service, the songs and the eulogy. But, she could not cry any longer. She was empty - empty of joy and full of sorrow.

Everyone who knew Hiawassee said the light went out of her eyes and the song left her heart the day Jacob died. Always a quiet woman, now she was silent most of the time. Her mighty pine was gone.

Chapter 15
Contact in the Dark of Night

1895 and years that followed

"Johnny," Hiawassee called from the front porch. "Will you come here a minute?"

John jumped up on the porch and joined his mother in the kitchen. She poured two cups of tea and brought a plate of biscuits to the table.

She looked tired and she moved slowly. "I have decided to move back to the little cabin," she said quietly as she sipped her tea.

"Why, Mama? This is where you and Papa lived most of your lives."

"Yes, but Jacob is gone. The house is large and I do not need this much space. It feels like the house is all around me, pinching me in and weighing me down. And, still it feels so empty." The window outside began to frost over as a cold wind blew in and deposited fluffy white clumps of snow all around.

"It's pretty out there isn't it?" Johnny said.

"It just looks cold to me," Rachel sighed.

"But, the cabin is so small, Mama," he protested.

"It has two rooms right now. I want you and your brothers to build a second cabin beside it with a dogtrot in the middle." The peppermint tea steamed as she continued to sip at it.

"We can make it nice for you, if you're sure that's what you want."

"It is. I can have my bedroom and sitting room with kitchen in the original side. The new cabin will be good for my spinning wheel and loom. The dogtrot, or center breeze-way between the two buildings, will be where I can hang and dry my herbs and beans. You boys can build a nice porch across the front, linking the two cabins."

"We can do that, Mama," he agreed.

"Many of my herbs are still there in the garden and I can plant clumps and clusters of other plants in the yard near the front door."

"It sounds like you have been thinking about this for a while." Johnny picked up a biscuit and bit off a bite.

"The path into the woods is still there and I know the mushrooms and moss I use are even closer to the door from the cabin than they are from here at the big house."

"Have you drawn up some plans too?" Johnny chuckled.

"No, just look at the first cabin and build one just like it, to the right, with a space of six feet in between for the dog-trot. The herbs will be both outside and inside, since the roof will span both cabins, the porch and the trot."

"And your pump organ?" Johnny asked.

"It will fit in the living side of the cabins." She picked up her cup and carried it to the dry sink. "I think I would like an in-door hand pump in the kitchen." She turned and looked beyond the room and to the barn yard. "The mornings are cold and the nights even colder."

Her sons began construction of the second cabin with logs they harvested from the woods. For every tree they removed, Hiawassee planted a new one. She would not have her cabin rob the woods of the scent and color that had always been there.

The boys completed the building and the loom and spinning wheel were set in their assigned places, but the rooms were silent most of the time.

The grandchildren, who had visited the house, but never the parlor, were soon in and out of her new home. They were her only callers. Because Rachel was so quiet, they were not frequent visitors. While Jacob lived, no one in the community talked to her and that did not change after his death.

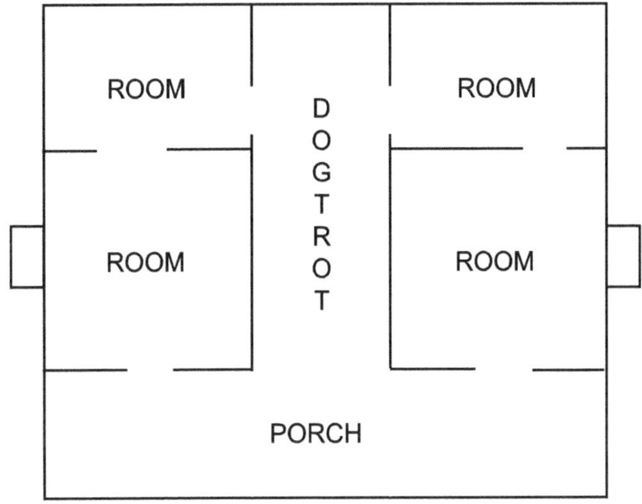

Pioneer Dogtrot House

The community's country doctor had been taken away and no one moved into the valley to take his place. But, they did have one person.

One night, like many nights, Hiawassee heard someone at the front door. *Tap, tap, tap.* The hour was late but it usually was. People did not show up at Rachel's cabin in the daylight. They didn't want anyone to see them talk to her or ask for her help.

"Yes, Grover," Rachel whispered when she opened the door. She did not even bring a lantern with her because she knew that whoever waited at the door would not want to be seen in the light.

"It's Becky, Ma'am." Grover hung his head as he pleaded for her help. "She's burnin' up with fever." He looked up at her, something he would never have done if he had seen her in town. "She's only eight." Tears ran down his face and dripped from his chin.

"Does she have a rash or spots?" Hiawassee asked as she threw her shawl around her shoulders.

"No, Ma'am." He wiped his nose on his sleeve and looked up again. "She's had stomach trouble though, throwing up and all."

"Is she in pain? Do her joints hurt or her head?"

"She's been complainin' of a headache. She's terrible weak, Ma'am. She's real wobbly when she walks."

"Has she eaten anything?"

"No. Her ma and I can only get a few sips of water in her."

She closed the door behind her to keep her cat inside. Out in the dogtrot, Rachel reached up and brought down some dried leaves. "Make a tea of these Chamomile leaves. It will calm her stomach and help her sleep. You can add a little of this dry Aspin for the fever. Keep cool compresses on her forehead, Grover."

"I'm thankin' ya, Ma'am." Grover clutched the herbs to his chest and slipped off in the darkness just as he had come.

Hiawassee was alone again. The stars lit the barnyard a little so she tarried in the night glow for a while. Johnny had placed two sturdy wooden rocking chairs on the porch and she slowly lowered herself into one of them.

She had always known that she could not change the strange world she had walked into with Jacob Meadows. She could only change herself, if change were needed.

In the land of the Cherokee, all are equal, all are

respected. That is the way of balance. Balance dictates that each end of the board must hold people of equal value. If the other end believed they were of more worth, Rachel would keep them in balance by believing the truth.

In her village in the Great Blue Ridge Mountains of North Carolina, no one came to someone's door by night and then turned their back on them in the light of day. She had resolved to treat everyone as her equal, even as a child. Prejudice and hate would be the other person's problem. It would eat away at their soul, but Hiawassee would choose love and balance.

She said nothing as she sat on the porch that night, since no one was around. But, she talked to God, alone in the dark, and she imagined that Jacob was by her side, rocking and inhaling the fragrance of the night.

Chapter 16
The Short Journey Home

Circa 1924

"But Mama, you are not as young as you were," Johnny protested as he loaded her spinning wheel and loom onto the wagon. He had taken care of Rachel for many years after Jacob died.

"None of us are," she agreed as she lifted material to be spun and threads for weaving onto the wagon.

"Not many of us are nearly one hundred and four," John snorted as he fussed with the barrels of material and boxes of clothes.

"Age is not a disease, Johnny. It is a fact of life." She repositioned her wheel to make sure it would not topple over as John drove her to Brown County where her family and tribe would gather for the annual encampment.

"Do you have your herbs?" John didn't wait for an answer. He seemed to be ticking off a list. "Salted pork, your dancing moccasins?"

"John Meadows, I do not dance any more. In fact, I do not wear shoes, you know that."

"Well, you won't be back until the spring. You know you'll need them in the cold weather." He laughed as he finished loading all of the things his mother took to reenact her lost life one more time.

"As much as I do not like to wear things on my feet, the cold weather does convince me." She chuckled a little along with him.

"What about all of the things you like to take to entertain your family? It is your time to share your best food and games. Goodness knows you haven't had any chance here in Heltonville."

"I do not believe that Goodness had anything to do with it." Rachel said with a little smile on her face.

"Mama, I think that's about the first time I ever heard you tell a joke." He gave her a little side-ways hug.

"Is it John?" She thought about it for a moment. "Well, for that I am sorry."

With everything ready, Rachel climbed up on the wagon seat with John's help. They bounced along on the dirt and gravel roads all the way to the encampment. As they drew near, children ran out to the edge of the road to greet Rachel. They all knew her story and were proud of her life of peace in the greater world outside of their village.

"Hiawassee is here!" they cheered. They chanted her name and danced beside the wagon until John pulled it to a stop. A person of age and wisdom, she was greatly respected. Everyone loved and admired her.

In the evening, the women danced in their full shirts and the men in headdresses of feathers. There were music and drums and laughter everywhere.

One morning, nearing the end of the encampment, in her one hundred and third year, Rachel Meadows did not wake up. Children came to her teepee first. They called out her name but she did not answer. It would not have been polite to go in. So, they ran to the other women in the tribe and told them they were worried. Rachel never overslept.

A celebration had been planned for that day. It would soon be time to go home and the tribe always threw a party to celebrate life and each one's connectedness within the tribe. Rachel had been looking forward to it.

"Come, she does not wake up," the children yelled.

A few of the women ran to her entrance and called out her name. "Hiawassee?" they spoke into the flap that covered the opening. "Are you alright?"

The women entered her teepee with heavy hearts. They feared what they would find. During the night, Rachel Meadows, Hiawassee, had slipped from her loneliness and back into the arms of her Jacob.

The tribe placed her gently on the ground, removed her heart and hung it by a piece of deer sinew from a red-bud tree, so the Great Spirit would be able to find her. Her body was taken back to Heltonville.

But, as in life, Rachel was not accepted into the resting place of Jacob and his people. Her children were forbidden to bury her in the family burial plot next to Jacob. She was laid to rest outside the Meadows' family cemetery, on a high and lonely hill.

Rachel would not have been sad. She would have been proud that she could bring peace to Jacob once more. Like a beam, poised on the fulcrum of God's love, she was the counterbalance for Jacob. Although trapped inside his family's circle, she was freely at rest, outside the circle, where Jacob had found peace.

Jacob had promised that someday, her people would be accepted in the church and community — the settlers' world. She knew that hate and prejudice can never win in the heart of God. Within God's arms is a place of acceptance and peace.

Rachel's Legacy
"Circles of Life"

"Circles of Life" is a ministry designed for Native Americans, serving people in the United States and Canada. It is located on the south east side of Indianapolis, Indiana on a five-acre original homestead.

Ron and Marilyn Haun have completely re-modeled one of the area's historical homes in order to provide outreach to Native Americans. A Sweat Lodge, bird center, community garden, which is over 6,000 square feet, and trails in the woods are all part of "Circles of Life."

The main attraction at "Circles of Life" is Rachel's Garden. The garden is named after Rachel Meadows and has over one hundred geode stones from the original land belonging to Jacob and Rachel. In addition, many of the plants that she loved are growing in her memory garden today.

The garden has been the setting for many gatherings, such as the Indiana School of Christian Missions for the United Methodist Women (now called Mission U). Throughout the year many area school children, scouting troops and various other organizations visit Rachel's Garden. In the fall of 2013, a traditional Native American wedding was celebrated in the arbor area of the Garden.

It is also in Rachel's Garden that many hospice patients spend a quiet afternoon. Not only do the patients enjoy being in the beauty of the garden but they also enjoy hearing the Native American flute music.

In the spring of 2014, Mormon missionaries spent six hours "spring cleaning" Rachel's garden, the first time that the Church of Latter Day Saints of Jesus Christ has volunteered gardening hours. The Mormon Church in Indianapolis is also in conversation about planting some flowers in the garden, donated by the two area churches, Fall Creek and Crossroads.

"Circles of Life" provides emergency housing, a food pantry, daily meals, and an area to wash and dry clothing, and the most important of all, a chance to be listened to, recognized and valued. Based upon the experiences of Rachel, it is well understood that everyone should be treated with respect and dignity. Acceptance is the main theme of the ministry.

"Circles of Life" is also in partnership and outreach with the Indiana Native American Committee of the United Methodist Church, as well as the Oklahoma Mission. Over five-hundred bags of clothing have been donated to the Miami Nation of Indians located in Peru, Indiana. The local Mormon churches have also helped with these donations, as well as loading and unloading trucks. With the help of several churches, a food pantry is being sponsored in Peru. The different churches also work together to help the children of the tribes. In 2014, one hundred twenty-five Easter baskets were made for the children of the Miami Nation by the pre-school classes at St. Andrew United Methodist Church, pastored by Ron Haun in Indianapolis.

Other organizations are also involved, such as the University of Indianapolis and I.U. Health Hospital. Student nurses are active in several outreach ministries.

"Rachel's Garden" also provides alter flowers to various churches. In the year 2013, the Community garden provided ten truckloads of fresh produce to area missions.

There is never a charge for any of the services provided at "Circles of Life." A speaker for a group presentation is also available at no cost.

"Circles of Life" had applied for a CORR Action Fund, sponsored by the General Commission on Religion and Race of the United Methodist Church. Rev. Anita Phillips, Executive Director of the Native American Comprehensive Plan, along with several other Native American Methodist groups, supported this vision. The first Native American "church plant" is being developed at the St. Andrew United Methodist Church in Indianapolis.

"I think Rachel would be pleased…don't you?"
Marilyn Ann Haun

For more information, please contact:
Rev. Ron and Marilyn Haun
Circles of Life
6125 Iona Road
Indianapolis, Indiana 46203

114

Places to Visit

New Echota: In 1825, the Cherokee Council named New Town, located at the headwaters of the Oostanaula River, the Cherokee Nation's capital. They renamed it New Echota, in honor of Echota, a Cherokee pioneer town. A community was developed there including, the Cherokee Council House, Supreme Court Building and Cherokee Phoenix Print Shop. After the removal of all Native Americans to lands west of the Mississippi, the town disappeared. It was restored in the 1950's. The New Echota State Historic Site was dedicated on May 12, 1962. It is located in northern Georgia.

Cherokee: Located in the heart of Western North Carolina, Cherokee is a sovereign nation. It is the ancestral home of the Cherokee people and continuous home of the Eastern Band of the Cherokee Nation. They are descendants of those who hid in the forest and mountains of North Carolina, rather than being driven off their land by the government. The Eastern Cherokee perform the reenactment: *Unto These Hills.*

The Cherokee Nation: The Capitol of the Cherokee Nation is located near Tahlequah, Oklahoma. The Cherokee Nation is the federally-recognized government of the Cherokee people. They have inherent sovereign status as stated by treaty and law. The Western Cherokee perform the reenactment: *Trail of Tears.*

In 1984 the first reunion since 1838 occurred between the Eastern and Western Cherokee. There were as many as thirty thousand Cherokee who celebrated the traditions and culture of their people. Hot coals from the sacred fire in the west that had been carried along the Trail of Tears were once again mixed with the sacred coals from the Eastern band. Then a new sacred fire was lit that would burn as long as the Principal People walked the earth.

CAUTION

The intent of this section is to offer historical uses of herbs and health foods. For up to date information, consult a well-researched book on herbs for their current use and warnings.

YOU SHOULD ALWAYS SPEAK WITH A HEALTH CARE PRACTITIONER BEFORE TAKING ANY DIETARY, NUTRITIONAL, HERBAL OR HOMEOPATHIC SUPPLEMENT.

Children: Herbs are not play food. Use only with the permission and supervision of parents and/or adults.

As with all kitchen spices and food: **KEEP HERBS OUT OF THE REACH OF CHILDREN.**

TERMS

Poultice [pohl-tis] Dictionary: a soft, moist cloth, bread, meal, herbs, etc. applied hot as a medicament to the body.

Hiawassee heated the herbs in hot water and spread them on a cloth. She applied the moist cloth with herbs to the sore area.

HERBS

Alfalfa — Native Americans used alfalfa to promote blood clotting, for arthritis, muscle problems, reduce blood sugar levels, eliminate toxins, increase energy, and for bone strength.

Allspice — Allspice was used to aid digestion and as an effective pain reliever along with dried, unripe berries in teas for treatment of colds, cramps, upset stomach, indigestion, and relief of muscle aches and pains. Crushed berries were used in poultices and salves and could be applied directly to bruises, sore joints, and aching muscles.

Bee Pollen — Bee pollen, mixed with food or drinks, was known as an energy source. It could act as an appetite suppressant, an aid in digestion, to strengthen the immune system, enhance memory and was also known to help with hay fever. Some people can be allergic to bee pollen.

Chamomile — Chamomile was made into a tea and it sometimes helped with sleep. It was also known to treat stomach and intestinal cramps and problems, nausea, and stomach flu. It was also an excellent calming agent and well suited for babies and children.

Chickweed — High in vitamins and minerals, the whole plant was used as an astringent, antihistamine, diuretic, and expectorant. Externally, poultices have been used to treat rheumatic pains, wounds, ulcers, roseola, itching skin conditions, cuts, minor burns, eczema, and rashes.

Dogwood — The Cherokee chewed the bark of the dogwood for headaches and used a decoction of bark to treat childhood afflictions such as worms, measles, and diarrhea. They also made poultices, which were used for wounds and other skin disorders. It has been proven to prevent the spread of malaria. The bark is rich in tannin and has been used as a substitute for quinine.

Evening Primrose — The Cherokee evening primrose was used for a number of purposes. The young roots can be eaten like a vegetable by putting the shoots in a salad. The whole plant was used in decoctions to treat asthma, cough disorders, and as a pain-killer. Poultices were also made to ease bruises, reduce swelling, and heal wounds. The Cherokee were known to cook the leave for greens and boil the roots like potatoes.

Galangal (ginger) — An herbal medicine, galangal has long been known for its warming and comforting effects on the digestion, similar to other ginger related herbs. Its mild spicy taste makes it a very soothing herb, used throughout the years to treat abdominal pain, vomiting, hiccups, diarrhea, flatulence, sore gums, and motion sickness.

Mint — Peppermint and other types of mint were made into tea and used as a stimulant for the stomach. They aided in digestion. Crushed and/or bruised leaves were made into cold compresses and salves, or were put in the bath water to relieve itching of the skin.

Quaking Aspen — Quaking aspen trees were used by Native Americans and early pioneers to treat fever, scurvy, cough, pain, and as an anti-inflammatory. The inner bark of this tree contains salicin, a substance similar to the active ingredient in aspirin.

Sage — White sage was used in "smudge sticks." Bundles of dry sage were burned slowly to make smoke. The smoke cleansed infected areas and brought relief to sufferers.

Skunkcabbage — Used to treat respiratory diseases, nervous disorders, rheumatism, and dropsy, skunkcabbage was not safe to eat raw. The leaves were dried and cooked into soups and stews.

Slippery Elm Bark — The inner side of the bark was dried and made into a powder. It was used to treat sore throat, cough, various digestive disorders, for wounds, burns, boils, and other external skin conditions.

Tassel Flower — Tassel flower was held in great regard as a poultice for cuts, bruises and as a treatment for cancer.

White Pine — The inner bark of white pine, young shoots, twigs, pitch, and leaves have long been used by Native Americans in medicinal remedies to treat colds, cough, flu, pneumonia, fever, heartburn, headache, arthritis, neuritis, bronchitis, croup, laryngitis, and kidney problems. Sometimes, the inner bark or the sap was used as a poultice for wounds and sores. Pitch was used to "draw out" boils, splinters, abscesses, and it was also used for rheumatism, broken bones, cuts, bruises, and inflammation. A hot resin was sometimes spread on a hot cloth and applied for the treatment of pneumonia, sciatic pains, and general muscular soreness.

 **About the Author: Doris Gaines Rapp**

"I first heard of Rachel Meadows when Marilyn Haun talked about her great-great-great grandmother, a Cherokee Indian, at a meeting of the Indiana Conference United Methodist Women. I was captured by Rachel's story of love and devotion, sacrifice and tragedy. When I called Marilyn to ask where I could buy her book for my granddaughter, she said there was none. What?! I had to write the book for Rachel, who, for me, will always be Hiawassee inside."

As an author, psychologist, former teacher, wife, mother and grandmother, Dr. Doris Gaines Rapp knows and understands Rachel from many perspectives. She was a woman of great strength, through her faith in God and her devotion to her husband and children. Doris hopes you will find a new spirit of God's power buried in your heart as you read her story.

Other books by Doris Gaines Rapp, all available at your local bookstore or on line:

Length of Days – The Age of Silence
Escape from the Belfry
Smoke from Distant Fires

Doris Gaines Rapp
P.O. Box 623
Huntington, Indiana 46750
dorisgainesrapp@gmail.com
www.dorisgainesrapp.com
www.prayertherapyrapp.blogspot.com

122

www.ingramcontent.com/pod-product-compliance
Lightning Source LLC
Chambersburg PA
CBHW070313120726
47910CB00007B/2471